Falling for Her Bachelor

Falling for Her Bachelor

The Bachelor Auction Returns

Robin Bielman

Falling for Her Bachelor

Tule Publishing First Printing, June 2016

The Tule Publishing Group, LLC

ISBN: 978-1-944925-75-8

Dedication

This one is for Elena Koutsi, reader, but more importantly, friend.

Acknowledgements

I had so much fun writing my first book for Tule and being part of the Montana Born Bachelor Auction series. Huge thanks to my dear friend and mentor, Charlene Sands, for asking me to join her in this series. Doing this together, Charlene, has been super special. xoxo

Thank you to Samanthe Beck for always being there to read, brainstorm, talk, and laugh. You're my rock.

Rachel Hamilton and Elena Koutsi, thanks so much for reading the first draft of Nick and Sid's story, and telling me just what I needed to hear. Your time and support are appreciated more than I can say. Love you girls!

Thank you to Meghan, Lindsey, Danielle, Laurie, Lee, Jane, and the entire Tule team. Hugs to Jeannie Moon and Sinclair Jayne, the other two awesome gals with bachelor auction books. I'm honored and so happy to be included in this series with you talented ladies.

Lots of love and thanks to my family.

And last, but never least, to my readers, new and old, thank you from the bottom of my heart for spending time with my characters. It means the world to me, and I hope for a little while I get to take you away and then leave you with a smile.

Chapter One

SOMETIMES PARADISE VALLEY looked like a Matisse painting had collided with a foreign planet. Cassidy Ware drew in a deep breath and stared in awe at the fusion of golden trees, snow-capped mountains, and emerald reeds among ice blue water. In all her travels, Montana still held the title of favorite place.

But not the place she should be anymore, her mind ventured.

She wished her thoughts would quit messing with her heart.

The stout, older man, fly-fishing half a football field away, struck the perfect pose and Cassidy once again lifted the camera around her neck. *Click, click, click*. She couldn't draw a proper stick figure to save her life, but behind a photo lens she always captured something magical.

From a young age, she'd satisfied her curiosity using her camera as a disguise, and while a part of her still believed that to be true, a bigger part of her now wanted to be seen as a person, not just a photographer. Change didn't happen overnight, but she'd promised herself she'd jump out of her comfort zone more often.

Digging her sneakers into the bank of the river, one foot slightly in front of the other, she continued to snap photos of the fly fisherman and surrounding beauty. Once satisfied, she took a step back, but with the ground overly saturated from recent rain, her foot slipped out from under her. She wavered, tried to catch herself with her arms out for balance, but, "crap!" failed when her other foot slid on the mud-slicked embankment.

Worried about her camera, she lifted it above her head and landed with a thud on her tailbone. Her shoes splashed into the frigid water. Muddy droplets hit her face. The sharp sting in her bottom made her wince.

But—she glanced up into the morning sun—her camera looked unharmed. She lowered her arms and exhaled in victory.

"Hey, you okay? That was a pretty nasty fall," someone said from behind her. A male someone with a seductive voice that brought to mind an image of tangled sheets and breakfast in bed.

Yep, it had been too long since she'd had a date when her mind raced there instead of feeling grateful for help if she needed it. *Thank you, Marietta.* If she were anywhere else but the safety of her hometown, old feelings of panic that still crept up on her occasionally might have lodged her heart into her throat instead.

She steeled herself a moment before turning to face the

man with the too-charming power of speech. "I'm okay."

The witness to her clumsiness moved closer, his frame blocking the sun over her shoulder. "Can I help you up?"

Cassidy inwardly sighed. The voice plus good manners took some of the sting out of her pain. And raised goose bumps on her skin. Or maybe that was the cold seeping into her jeans. Besides the chilly water, spring had only recently chased winter away, and today's temp lingered around fifty-five degrees.

"Sure, thank you." She turned to her Good Samaritan. "Nick?" she said surprised.

He squinted as his arms moved under hers to hoist her up. "Sid?"

She bristled at the nickname only he used. They hadn't seen each other since he left to join the navy after graduating from high school, but apparently some things never changed. His sister, Rowan, had told her he was in town after being honorably discharged and she'd figured, now that they were adults, he'd quit with the boy name he knew annoyed her. Guess not.

"The one and only," she said.

Her foot skidded in the muddy bank and his hold on her tightened. Not sure what to do with her arms, she wrapped them around his middle. Her camera pressed into her stomach, but she'd rather that than be hip to hip.

He took all her weight and moved them back to safer ground. His midnight blue eyes, fringed with dark black lashes, held her gaze, their confidence and magnetism a double dose of trouble. He'd always been comfortable looking people—especially girls—right in the eye.

"There you go," he said, taking a big step back. Did she smell or something? He wiped his long sleeve across his forehead and that was when she took in his whole appearance. Running shorts, running shoes, a sweaty T-shirt, his black hair curled with perspiration at his neck. "Probably don't want to stand too close," he added.

Happy to hear the distance had nothing to do with her, she said, "Thanks." Then without her permission her eyes took one more peek at his very nice muscular legs before landing back on his face. A face that had only gotten better looking with age. "Sorry I interrupted your run." *And for the record you smell really good.*

"I'm not."

Her heart rate sped up.

"I'm damn tired and you supplied the perfect excuse to stop running."

Her heart rate slowed down.

"You didn't answer me before. Are you okay?"

She rubbed her backside. "Nothing a little aspirin and warm bath can't cure." At least she *hoped* that would heal her pain. Her tailbone seriously felt on fire.

Nick studied her like "warm bath" in reference to her didn't compute. Her teenage daydreams might have starred him in various rooms of her house in various degrees of undress, but he'd never looked at her as anything other than a pesky "little sister" and Rowan's best friend.

Cassidy had never admitted to anyone her huge crush on him. Not that he would have been the least bit interested if he'd known. Back in high school, Nick Palotay was one of Marietta's star football players, had enough charisma to reach all four corners of the state, and looked like a movie star. Every girl who laid eyes on him had swooned. And he'd loved every second of the attention.

"That's good to hear. Come on, I'll walk you to your car," he said.

She took two steps forward and had to stop to catch her breath. Holy magnum mackerel, her ass hurt. Maybe she'd just stay right where she stood. Snap more pictures.

Before she had time to protest or realize his intentions, Nick scooped her up into his arms. "Hey! What are you—*ouch*—doing? Put me down!"

"Relax, Sid Vicious. This way will be less painful to your delicate derriere."

"Did you just say derriere?" she asked, definitely relaxing now.

She couldn't remember the last time a guy had lifted her off her feet, probably because it had never happened. Would it be rude of her to squeeze his biceps, just to, you know, see what they felt like?

"I did. And if you tell anyone I'll deny it." He smiled then, his straight, white teeth on perfect display, and a pleasant and unwelcome ache sparked to life between her hips.

Embarrassment burned her cheeks. She tucked her chin into her neck. Because really? Nick had to be the first guy to make her body tingle in forever? Her crush long over, he was her best friend's brother. Nothing more.

"Still taking pictures, I see," he said, walking them away from the river.

"I'm a freelance photographer."

"With a penchant for fly fishermen?"

She raised her eyes to meet his. "People, actually. Doing everyday and extraordinary things. I work for several prestigious publications and travel more often than not. I'm considering leaving Marietta to make home base New York or LA actually." Why she felt the need to defend herself she didn't know. Or maybe it was just that she wanted to impress him. Which was ridiculous. She didn't care what he thought of her. Didn't care if she laid eyes on him again after today.

"I always knew you'd be successful at it."

"You did?" He'd thought about her that way?

"Yeah, anyone who could annoy me as much as you did with all the '*say cheese!*' was going to do well with it."

Cassidy ground her teeth together before hitting him in the chest. A chest she couldn't help but notice had definition beneath the cotton barrier. "Jerk."

He chuckled. "I've been called worse."

"Says the current hero." Marietta loved their local heroes like nobody's business and it was no secret Nick had saved several fellow navy officers during a sub fire last month. Rowan had told her he'd also lost his two closest friends. "I'm, uh, sorry for your loss."

His jaw tensed. "Thanks, but I'm not a hero."

"That's not—" She sealed her lips when he glared at her. Who knew eyes as gorgeous as his could look so intimidating?

They continued in silence, the patch of dirt she'd parked her car on coming into view up ahead. Another runner came toward them on the dirt trail. He nodded and shared a "good morning" as they crossed paths.

"Morning," she said in return, adding extra cheer into the single word. She didn't like the tension suddenly rolling off Nick and thought to break it.

"Think you could quit wiggling?" His gruff tone indicated she hadn't broken a damn thing.

"Sorry, what?" She squirmed, purposely playing dumb and trying to irritate him, but inadvertently rubbing the side of her chest against his at the same time. *You should really plan more carefully next time.*

Next time?

That was totally her boob talking.

"I guess your fall affected your hearing, too?" By the vexed look on his chiseled face he knew she'd heard him loud and clear.

"Guess so."

"Maybe you should tie a pillow around your waist to prevent further injury the next time you fall on your ass."

Cassidy didn't like his implication that she was accident prone, but the comment held deeper meaning that lifted the corners of her mouth. "You remember Rowan and I used to do that?" When she and Ro were around five and learning to skate, they'd tied pillows around themselves to cushion their many falls.

"Kind of hard to forget when for one summer I never had a pillow on my bed." His voice held irritation, but also a hint of affection. Cassidy wondered if all their recollections would be less maddening now that they were older. Wiser.

She thought back to that day in the Palotay kitchen when she was fourteen, telling Rowan how nervous she was about having her first kiss. Besides the fact that her parents would ground her for life if they'd found out she liked a boy at school well enough to want to kiss him, she didn't know the first thing about kissing. Nick had come into the kitchen and overheard their conversation. "I can fix that," he said all calm, cool, and experienced at sixteen. He'd walked over to her, kissed her right on the mouth, and stepped back. "Still nervous?" he'd asked and then he walked away as if he hadn't just stolen her first kiss like it was no big deal.

The least he could have done was add some tongue, Cassidy thought now, smiling inwardly at the memory rather than think anything childish about it. Her virgin lips had tingled for *hours* after that kiss.

Nick stopped and lowered her down next to her old, but reliable, Volvo. "Thanks for the lift," she said, wishing she had a pillow in her car to cushion her backside while she drove home. "Can I give you a ride?"

"Nah. I'm better off finishing my run."

"Yeah, I can see that," she said, waving her finger up and down his body to draw attention to his unfair physique. If only she had x-ray vision so she could confirm whether or not he had a six-pack hiding underneath his shirt.

He tossed her an overconfident smile. *Uh-oh.* "What can you see, Sid?"

"Oh, you know, that you're slacking on your cardio."

"Still afraid to say what's really on your mind, huh?"

"What? I am not." Just because she kept her thoughts to herself didn't mean she was afraid. Her overprotective parents had drilled caution and modesty into her. Molded her into a careful, quiet observer.

"Prove it." He tossed out with that cocky attitude she remembered him flaunting when they were younger.

"I don't need to prove anything to you."

"Not to me. To yourself."

His too-keen observation set off shivers in places she didn't know she could shiver. Had he always noticed that about her? Or had he developed some ninja military skill that allowed him to read people in all of fifteen minutes? Didn't matter. No way was she letting him win this little challenge.

He'd won every single one of them when they were kids.

Plus, she wanted to shed that suffocating part of her personality. Had been working on it since she'd made a resolution months ago to walk on the wild side more often.

Nick Palotay equaled wild. A safe wild because she knew he'd never harm her. Although just looking at him kind of hurt. He took eye candy to a whole new level.

She opened her car door, lifted her camera from around her neck, and put it in its case on the back seat. "I see a lot of things, Nick. As a professional photographer, I'm trained to see what other people don't."

"You still haven't answered my question," he said smugly.

"Fine. I see"—she turned and crossed her arms over her chest—"a good looking guy who…would be perfect for the charity firemen's calendar I've been asked to help with. You fly fish? We could put you in some waders and nothing else. You'd have women *angling* to get in those pants for sure." She pressed her lips together in a pleased-with-herself smile.

Nick looked ready to run all the way to Canada. "Oh, hell no." He slid a couple of fingers inside the collar of his shirt to pull the material away from his neck. "There are plenty of other guys—"

Cassidy cracked up. "I'm joking. Mr. July is already taken."

He scowled.

"Kidding. There's no calendar." And then because she

loved seeing him disgruntled *and* sexy, added, "yet."

His expression changed then, to something she'd never seen directed at her before. Admiration, she thought, like he was impressed she'd teased him. Put a check in the Cassidy column.

"See you around, Sid."

"Yeah. Good luck tonight." She uncrossed her arms and opened the driver's side door.

"Tonight?"

"The Bachelor Auction?"

"Right." He stepped closer so his arm rested on the top of the car window while she carefully sat inside. Mother of Pearl her tailbone smarted.

"I'll be there to eat and drink since the proceeds are going toward Coach D's fundraiser as well. Plus, your sister told me if I stayed home by myself while I was in town that she'd do something drastic like post my picture to a dating website."

"Funny, she told me if I offered a boring date she'd post my picture to a dating website."

"I didn't think boring was in your genetic make-up."

He shrugged. "I guess I'll see you later."

"Maybe. Word has it Grey's will be packed tonight. Standing room only." Which worked in her favor given it felt awful to sit at the moment. "Thanks for coming to my rescue."

"Sure." He shut her door, took off at a brisk pace down

the dirt trail. She watched him until he disappeared from sight before turning the key in the ignition.

She might be at the saloon later, but she planned to keep her distance from Nick. He'd starred in all her teenage dreams, and that was where she'd keep him. Because today, the minutes with him in particular, had felt different for the first time in forever, and that scared the junk out of her.

Chapter Two

THE AMOUNT OF people in Grey's Saloon surely broke fire code, but considering the reason they were all there, and the fact that several emergency medical professionals were having a drink at the bar, Nick Palotay let the discomfort roll off his back.

Tonight was about Coach Downey and raising the remaining funds needed to build a lighted, heated, deicing helipad on the roof of Marietta Regional Hospital. A year and a half ago, Coach's grandson, Troy, had been critically injured during the high school's final football game. He'd been airlifted off the field with heavy snow falling and flown to the medical center in Bozeman. Those extra minutes of travel because Marietta Regional couldn't accommodate a safe emergency landing had been the difference between life and death.

Nick remembered with vivid clarity Troy as a little boy running onto the football field during his high school practices. He, Cody, Gavin, and Colt had made the kid their special mascot, tossing him on their shoulders and teaching him how to catch a football. Troy loved the game as much as they did and he'd made varsity his freshman year. The star running back blew all previous records—including Nick's—out of the water. College scholarship offers started pouring in his junior year. Coach D's emails to Nick were full of pride and affection for his grandson.

After hearing about the accident and Troy's passing, Nick had hit the gym and punched the living hell out of the punching bag. For Coach and his family. But also for himself, because it reminded him of his own devastating loss. His high school girlfriend, Sloane, never left the back of his mind. He'd ditched his own football scholarship to join the navy, choosing firefighting because of her. And just last month he'd lost his two best friends, Jake and Alex, to a sub fire. They'd died in battle, while he'd survived and been deemed a hero.

Honorably discharged from the navy, he was back in Marietta temporarily to help Coach with his bachelor auction, celebrate his dad's sixtieth, and figure out what he wanted to do with the rest of his life. He didn't know if he could be around fire again. Losing Jake and Alex had changed him. They were more than friends. They were brothers.

"There you are!" Rowan said, weaving through the crowd. "What are you doing standing here at the entrance?" Hands on her hips, she gave him the I-may-be-younger-but-don't-mess-with-me face she'd perfected when they were kids.

"I just walked in."

"Five minutes late." She looked him up and down. "I'll forgive you because you look good."

"Just good?"

Rowan rolled her eyes. She'd appointed herself style-maker for this evening, telling him exactly what to wear in order to bring in the most cash. A few days ago, she'd made a friendly bet with Lily Taylor, the woman who had arranged a bachelor auction last year, that this time they'd raise more money. Rowan's competitive streak took over after that, and his fellow bachelors—and close high school football friends—had started calling her drill sergeant.

"More than good and you know it. We are going to kick ass tonight," she said with the winsome smile he'd missed while away. "Come on. Coach and the other victims"—she winked at him over her shoulder—"I mean bachelors are upstairs."

Back in high school, Nick would have loved attention from a room full of women, but it didn't quite hold the same appeal at thirty. He'd work it, though. He hadn't lost his charm and certainly wasn't shy.

They walked past the bar, Nick slapping search and rescue head of operations, Flynn Benson, on the back. A couple other SAR personnel nodded. Nick had been in town a week and met Flynn for the first time the other day. A former hot shot for the National Forestry Agency, Nick had thought Flynn could offer some insight into the National Interagency

Fire Center. The NIFC wanted Nick on their team in Idaho. He had a month to tell them yes or no.

"Oh, my God! Oh, my God! Nick Palotay!" A woman squealed. Yes, squealed. So piercing that, no doubt, the entire saloon heard his name over their conversations.

Nick turned his head to find a woman he didn't recognize throw herself at him. He managed to extract her before her arms locked around his neck.

"Hi, gorgeous." The smell of bourbon hit him in the face. "I am sooooo excited to see you."

Not wanting to be rude, he said a simple, "Hi," in return.

"It's Mandy." That didn't ring any bells. She waved her hand in dismissal. "You probably remember me as Amanda. Amanda Pryce."

He tried not to wince. Of course he remembered her. She'd stalked him in high school. Nothing mean-spirited or overly worrisome, just fanatical and hard-core devoted, even when he had a girlfriend.

"Right. Amanda. How are you?" He glanced to the side. Rowan finally realized he wasn't beside her and had turned around, her eyes widening when she saw Amanda invading his personal space.

"I'm soooo good. I'm gonna win you tonight."

"Oh?" Hell no. The thought of spending the weekend with Amanda put every muscle in his body on high alert. It was bad enough Rowan had shot down his idea for a laidback weekend of wine tasting and art galleries in favor of an adrenaline fueled adventure—her words, not his. So much for his playing it safe and keeping his mind off another person's well-being for a while.

Amanda put her hand on his chest. He took her wrist and placed her arm back at her side. "I've got thousands to spend on you, big boy. You. Are. Mine."

"Hey, Mandy," Rowan said, finally reaching them. "I need to get my brother ready to go on stage. Have fun tonight." She took Nick's hand and spun them away before Amanda could say anything else disturbing.

When they reached the stairs leading up to the storage room that was serving as tonight's makeshift dressing room, Nick pulled Ro to a stop. "You cannot let Amanda Pryce win me tonight."

"What?"

"She said she's prepared to win me. You can't let that happen. The woman is..."

"Still off her rocker. I know. But what can I do?"

He scanned the room. "Ask someone else to win the date."

Ro put her hand on his arm. "Nick, there's a ton of people here tonight, but not a lot of them can afford to bid like Mandy can. At least not without pissing off their husbands."

"I'll cover it."

"What do you mean, you'll cover it?" She eyed him warily. They didn't keep secrets from each other.

Except one. One secret Nick hadn't told a soul. An image of Sloane, so pretty in a white sundress with tiny blue flowers, flashed in his mind. He always pictured the last time he saw her when thinking about her now.

"Jake left me half a million dollars. I only found out last week." His navy buddy hadn't any immediate family, his parents passing away several years ago and leaving him a nice inheritance. One that now belonged to Nick. He wasn't sure how he felt about it, but giving money to tonight's event was something his best friend would have happily done.

Fuck. His chest hurt sharing that news. Not a day passed that he didn't wish things had gone differently. It wasn't the first time their crew had faced volatile conditions. They knew the danger. But once in a while containing hazardous situations didn't end in their favor.

"Wow."

"Yeah. So my bidder can go as high as she wants. As high as she needs to." He corrected.

Rowan tapped her chin. "I think I know just the person."

"Palotay, get yourself up here," Coach said from the stair railing. "We're waiting on you. I've got a pep talk to give."

Nick smiled, his shoulders relaxed. "On my way," he called up.

"I'll just go find your rescuer and then I'll be up to give you guys *my* pep talk." She straightened the collar on his white button down. "Mine has to do with channeling Channing Tatum."

He cringed at the thought. "Thanks for the save, Ro."

"No worries. This just means you have to do my interview now." She waved her fingers over her shoulder and took off.

She'd been on him about a piece for the *Copper Mountain Courier* since he'd arrived. She usually covered the sports beat, but had been given the go-ahead to write a story on him. Other local media wanted interviews, too. But he wanted to keep attention off his occupation and "hero" label. He wasn't a hero. He was just doing his job.

A certain green-eyed photographer from this morning came to mind. He'd come to Cassidy's rescue and it had felt good. *She* had felt good. He'd almost groaned when she purposely wiggled in his arms. Which completely threw him off balance. Sid had never registered on his female antennae, not the way she once secretly wanted. She'd had a crush on him growing up, he knew, but he always thought of her like a kid sister, bugging him quietly while Ro bugged him loudly.

Today, though, he hadn't looked at her like a sister.

Her green eyes had always been pretty, but now they sparkled with life. She'd seen things, done things, in the past dozen years, and interest had flickered deep inside his chest. Then he'd noticed how sexy the messy bun on top of her head was, the fine slopes of her cheeks, her full mouth.

A mouth he'd pictured… *Don't go there, Palotay.*

He took the stairs two at a time, telling himself guys naturally thought of pretty, pink lips wrapped around their dicks. The image didn't mean anything. She might have looked at him with interest, but that didn't mean he'd take advantage it.

Stress over deciding his next career step had him thinking all sorts of strange things, that was all. And until he made a decision and sorted through the crap in his head, he'd probably ponder a few more never-going-to-happen scenarios.

"*YOU KNOW WHAT they say about doctors.*"

"No, what?"

"They're excellent with their hands."

"Gavin Clark might be good with his hands, but I guarantee you Nick Palotay is good with his hands *and* his mouth."

Cassidy tugged on her earlobe as she listened to the two young, pretty teachers from Marietta High on the barstools beside her talk about the guys on the auction block tonight.

"If we put our money together we might be able to win his date. There's no rule that says a bachelor can't make it a threesome," the blonde said, her voice taking on a kittenish quality Cass had tried to practice in the mirror once. She'd sounded like a kitten held under the devil's armpit.

"Hey, Cass," Reese said from behind the bar, "another pineapple juice?"

"No, thanks. I'm good." She shook the ice in her tumbler before setting the glass aside.

"Flag me down if you change your mind." He tapped the bar and turned, orders coming at him with every step away.

Cass wheeled around to lean against the smooth wood counter. She'd made herself comfortable standing almost in shadow at the end of the bar. It allowed her a clear view of the stage without bringing attention to herself. More than one friend tonight had already asked whom she planned to bid on. "Not sure," she'd answered, because it was easier than saying "none."

You could bid if you wanted to. She glanced down at the program in her hand. Nick, Cody Matthews, Gavin Clark, and Colt Ewing were each offering impressive dates. Cass knew with certainty Ro would win her little side bet with Lily, sending another nice chunk of change—literally—Coach's way.

"I knew I'd find you in this exact spot," Rowan said, appearing as if Cassidy's thought had conjured her.

"What's up?"

Rowan looked down the bar with a smile at the high school teachers. "I have to pee," she said, grabbing Cassidy's hand and hauling her toward the restroom. She stopped in the empty hallway. "I need your help."

Cass scrunched up her nose. "Peeing?" She'd do anything for Ro, just wanted some clarification.

"No, goofy, with the auction."

"O-kay," Cassidy said. Rowan had that twinkle in her eye that made her scary and beautiful at the same time.

"Actually, it's not me that needs the help, but Nick." She glanced at the watch on her wrist. "I need to make this quick so the gist is you need to bid on and win his date to save him from Mandy."

"Crazy Mandy?"

Ro nodded. "She's still in love with him and he's freaking out at the idea of spending a weekend with her."

"I would be, too."

"Exactly. So will you do it? It's actually a great idea anyway."

"What do you mean anyway?" A weekend away with Nick was so not a great idea, no matter that her insides were currently rocking a confetti party.

"You've been craving some adventure and this is your chance to get out from behind your camera for a weekend and have fun. You and Nick are like siblings so you can both let loose and have a great time without worrying about anything sexual going on.

"Plus, he's safe," Ro said softly. "You can trust him to take good care of you. And I can trust you to take good care of him. He's still reeling from losing his friends in the sub fire and could use time away without having to worry about his date planning their wedding."

Everything Ro said made perfect sense. Lonely and restless, Cass did want an adventure, and to do so with a man she could trust gave her the chance to be carefree without worry. A chance to step out of that box keeping her stuck. She'd just ignore Nick's good looks and the way her body liked to perk up when around him.

"Okay. I'll do it."

Rowan clapped her hands together and tucked them under her chin. "Thank you. He'll be so relieved when I tell him. Oh, and I almost forgot. He's got the bid covered so go as high as you have to."

Cass had forgotten about the money part of this plan. "Is that allowed? I can—"

"There aren't any written rules that I know of. Besides, following rules all the time is boring and didn't you tell me just the other day that you were tired of boring?"

"Yes." Cass relented. Nick's auction date included a weekend away to Jackson Hole with skydiving, hot springs, a wildlife safari by jeep, and fine dining. Excitement coursed through her picturing an entire weekend with the boy of her teenage dreams. How many women got to do something like that?

"Great." Ro wrapped her arms around Cass in a warm, sisterly hug. "Remember, money's no object. Just win."

"Gotcha," she said to Rowan's retreating back.

Then she took a deep breath, in through her nose, out through her mouth. Given Ro was in a hurry, she hadn't told her best friend the other reason she'd agreed to do this. Helping Nick meant he owed her one, and, she suddenly realized, she could use a favor in return.

At the end of the month, she had a black tie photography association dinner to attend in Helena and bringing a date would save her from the unwanted advances of a fellow photographer. Jesse had asked her out repeatedly, but she wasn't interested in anything more than friendship with him. And even that was getting harder since he continued to pursue her whenever their paths crossed.

With Nick by her side for the evening, she'd be able to relax and enjoy herself rather than worry about trusting Jesse to keep his distance.

Growing up, Cassidy's parents had taught her to give her trust only to those who earned it. They'd lectured her on being cautious and avoiding risky situations. "It's okay to say no," her mom said all the time, proving it by forbidding Cass to do so many things her friends were allowed to do. Like go to parties and concerts or clothes shopping in Bozeman. Her only saving grace had been sleepovers at Rowan's house. In college, though, out from under the thumb of her overprotective parents for the first time, she'd felt like she could finally spread her wings. She dated, joined a sorority, went to frat parties. And trusted the wrong person. Only Rowan knew what had happened that horrible night.

Cass shivered involuntarily. She hated that the past still affected her present. It wasn't that she immediately had doubts about every man she met. She'd had two boyfriends since college. Safe, uninspiring, vanilla guys that helped her get comfortable with the opposite sex again. But deep down she wanted to be a little reckless. Not that she was into anything kinky. She just yearned for sex that rocked her world with a man who placed passion over pragmatism.

She and Nick wouldn't get physical, but they could have a blast together. His fearless, devil-may-care mentality came wrapped in a protective bow. He proved safety and adventure could go hand in hand. A weekend with him was exactly what she needed to unleash the gutsy side of her she never gave freedom to.

She didn't relish the situation, didn't want it to seem like her help rose from a need of her own. But she and Nick were "family" and family did stuff like this without guilt, right? As an only child, Cass had nothing to go by.

Voices from the main room of the saloon grew louder, whistles sounded. *Showtime.*

Cassidy hurried out of the hallway, squeezing in at a table with some friends seated front and center when they waved her over. No more blending into the background.

Coach Downey stood up on stage, thanked the crowd for their support, and thanked everyone involved behind the scenes. He introduced Cody then started the bidding at five hundred dollars. The crowded saloon turned into a lively bidding war until Hayley O'Malley, a big, Hollywood movie star now, won the date with a huge sum of money.

Next up was Cass's bachelor.

The second Nick appeared on stage, the saloon went

wild. Cass got a little light-headed and warm at the same time, a fluttery current of awareness threading through her body. All the hundreds of times she'd considered him in her youth paled in comparison to the way she regarded him now.

He. Was. Hot. He wore a crisp white button-down with the top two buttons open, khaki pants, and black military boots that were untied. The mix of dressy and casual really worked. For some strange reason, his loose shoelaces put quivers in the pit of her stomach.

And the way he swaggered across the stage with a smile that put all other smiles to shame sent a rush of unfamiliar sensations to the parts of her body long neglected and aching for attention.

This was bad.

Bad can be very, very good.

Lost in inappropriate thoughts, she missed his introduction and the first few shout-outs of bids. The look of dread on Nick's face brought her back to her senses. Mandy called out a number, a really high number with lots of zeroes.

"Nine thousand." Cassidy announced.

The room fell silent. All eyes landed on her. Including Nick's. Cass couldn't look at him so turned to her girlfriends' surprised expressions. She'd never made such a bold move before in her life so their shock was understandable.

"Ninety-two hundred," Mandy shouted.

"Ninety-four," Cass said.

"Ninety-six." Mandy jumped to her feet, sending Cassidy an evil glare.

Cass almost laughed at being put in this unexpected situation. She never could have predicted being in a bidding war for Nick Palotay and finding it fun, exhilarating, worth all the attention on her.

"Ninety-nine," Cass said with a firmness she hoped begged no further opposition. Ninety-nine had been Nick's jersey number. It seemed fitting to stop there given it was football that brought them here tonight.

The resigned look in Mandy's eyes told Cassidy she got it and, with shoulders sagging, she sat back down in quiet defeat. Cassidy mustered the courage to look back up on stage.

"Going once. Going twice. Sold for nine thousand nine hundred dollars to Miss Cassidy Ware!"

Cass gave a curt nod before finding Nick's gaze zeroed in on her like a laser beam. Was he happy? Relieved? Nope, neither of those things, she decided. Because his eyes said something that made her want to run and hide. His royal blues whispered she was in over her head.

Chapter Three

"WHAT WERE YOU thinking having Sid bid on me?" Nick asked, pacing around the small dressing room. The auction over, he needed a minute alone with his sister before they joined everyone downstairs.

"Uh…that I was doing just what you asked." Rowan didn't need to add *dumbshit* at the end of her answer. He heard it loud and clear in her tone.

He stopped moving and met the annoyed, pinched line of her mouth. "I didn't want to exchange one problem for another."

Ro's baby blues, already big and round, grew bigger and rounder. "What in the world are you talking about? You cannot possibly compare Cass to Manic Mandy. You do remember who Cass is, right? You didn't suffer some head trauma in the sub fire, did you? Because you are talking crazy-pants right now."

Nick clenched his hands. "I know exactly who Cassidy is and exactly what I'm saying."

"No, you don't. Because Cass is the best person I know. She is good inside and out and *problem* is the very last word anyone would associate with her."

He opened his mouth to speak, but Ro cut him off before he could get a word out.

"She did you a huge favor tonight and you're sulking around like it's the end of the world. She spent almost ten thousand dollars on you!"

"Of my money."

Rowan threw her arms in air. "Oh, my God."

"You could have asked anyone."

"And I asked the person I thought—no, know—was best." She shook her head and studied the floor like she thought him a total idiot. It wasn't the first time he'd gotten this kind of reaction from her. "What's really going on here?" she said, raising her chin and searching his face.

"Truth?"

"That would be nice."

He slid his hands into the front pockets of his pants. "I think she still has a crush on me and that's a problem."

Rowan laughed. "What are you talking about? Cass is so not into you. She never was."

"You're wrong," he said confidently.

"I think I know my best friend. She's hated you ever since you put a snake in her sleeping bag when we were seven and camping out in the backyard."

Nick had forgotten about that. He'd caught the harmless gopher snake earlier in the evening and, being nine and tough, he'd wanted to show off a little. Plus, the girls hadn't invited him to make s'mores and he'd been upset about that. He hadn't anticipated making Cassidy cry, though. When he tried to apologize she told him she hated him.

"She outgrew it." Sid had developed the classic look of infatuation he'd read on lots of girls' faces, starting in middle school and continuing through high school, with little encouragement on his part.

"I'll buy she stopped hating you, and I know girls have always fallen all over themselves for you, but sorry to burst that big ego of yours, Cass thinks of you like an older brother and nothing more."

"I guarantee you there's more to it than that, and the last thing I want is a weekend away with her if she's hoping to get some sort of romantic relationship out of the date."

Someone cleared her throat from over his shoulder. Shit. He hadn't meant to be overheard and spun around, ready to do damage control. Only there was no defending himself against the woman standing in the doorway with a look of...well, hate in her pretty green eyes.

"Nick Palotay, if you were the last man on the planet, I still wouldn't want a romantic relationship with you." Cassidy announced.

"Told you," Rowan said from behind him.

He rubbed the back of his neck. He hadn't been wrong. Trouble stood right there ten feet away from him wearing form-fitting jeans, a pale yellow sweater, and cowboy boots.

"How long have you been standing there?" he asked.

"Long enough." She fired back.

Nick turned so he could address his sister without giving his back to Cassidy. "You mind going downstairs so I can talk to Sid?"

"I don't mind if she doesn't mind." Rowan had always protected Cassidy with sisterly support so her answer didn't surprise him. Come to think of it, Ro asking Cassidy to bid on him shouldn't have come as a surprise either.

"It's fine," Sid said. "It's going to be a short conversation."

The two women shared a quick hug as they passed each other. "Sorry about grumpy over there," Ro said. "You were awesome tonight. Thanks for *saving his ass.*" She cut him a quick glare, which he supposed he deserved.

"No problem," Cassidy said.

Rowan lit up like a sparkler on the Fourth of July at that comment, her glare disappearing and a smug expression taking its place. Ro didn't see his dilemma, but being with Sid for a weekend *was* a problem. Attraction or not aside, he didn't want to spend forty-eight hours in close proximity with anyone he was friendly with. Friends thought it okay to ask questions. Pry. Ask him to share shit he didn't want to talk about. He'd slammed the door shut on getting too personal with anyone, but ten minutes with Cassidy this morning and he'd called her out on her crush. *That* had surprised the hell out of him. And he didn't like feeling out of control of his actions.

"Keep it amicable you two," Ro said with a wave over her shoulder as she disappeared from the room.

Sid faced him, and in a very uncharacteristic move, tilted her head just a little to the side to contemplate him like she could reach into his soul and pluck out all his secrets. He dropped his gaze to the floor. What the hell?

"We don't have to go on the date," she said. No anger. No disrespect. Only kindness accompanied her words.

Nick didn't want her kindness.

"The point was to save you from Mandy and give money to a really good cause. There's no reason we have to follow through. No one's going to check up on us."

He also didn't want her taking the high road. He'd agreed to take part in the auction and, yeah, the money raised mattered most, but he didn't back out of something he promised. "I offered a weekend in Jackson Hole and I'm going to follow through."

"And be miserable?"

"I never said I'd be miserable." More like restless. Guarded.

She crossed her arms over her chest, accentuating the generous, round swells there. "Now who's afraid to say what's really on his mind?"

Oh, so she thought she could use a little reverse psychology on him, did she? He stepped forward, shrinking the space between them. "Says the eavesdropper."

"I had something in my boot. I was trying to get it out."

Nick laughed. Sid had never been this quick to go toe-to-toe with him when they were younger. "What was it?"

"I told you. Something."

"Does this something have a name?"

"If it had a name I would have used it instead of saying something."

He watched in fascination as she pressed her lips together in an effort to keep from smiling and exposing her lie. They both knew she wasn't telling the truth but it was fun to pretend.

"Are you available next weekend?" He inched backward, reminding himself to keep their conversations fun-free.

"I think so. I'll have to double check my calendar."

"Good. We'll leave Friday morning."

"You don't have to do this."

The cadence of her voice needled at him. He hadn't always been a man of honor in his impulsive youth, but he was now. "Yeah, I do. I want to. Just keep in mind this is a business transaction and nothing more."

"I'm glad you put it that way."

"You are?" No way had he read her wrong. Her chin might be lifted in defiance, but the rapid pulse at the base of her neck gave her away.

"Yes." She put her hand on his chest. A move he had no idea what to make of. Apparently he hadn't stepped back far enough. "I need a favor from you and figure you can't say no now."

"You agreed to bid on me so I'd return the favor?" He didn't entirely buy it.

"Yep." She dropped her hand.

"So, you're not looking forward to what I have planned at all?" Why that bothered him, he didn't know. Her indifference should make him happy.

She thought on that for a long damn time before she said, "I think I should plead the fifth on that."

"Why?"

"Because it doesn't matter."

But it did matter. Nick wanted Cassidy to enjoy herself and if she had reservations about any of the activities, he could modify them. Which meant he wasn't as unaffected by their situation as he needed to be. He'd want whoever had won his date to have a good time, but seeing the intelligent, yet vulnerable look in this particular woman's eyes, he knew she upped the stakes.

"OKAY," NICK SAID. "What's this favor you want from me?"

That's all this is about, one good turn for another. He'd successfully abolished any fondness she had for him with his conceited use of the word *problem.* And an ego big enough to squeeze all the air out of the room.

Or maybe the hard to breathe thing had more to do with the soft waves in his dark hair, the way his lips moved when he talked, and the way he smelled like a warm summer night even though the calendar said April.

Whatever. She could appreciate his appearance and not engage her heart or head.

"I have a dinner to attend at the end of the month and could use a date."

"Because?"

She pressed her hand against her jean-clad thigh to stop her foot from tapping. "There's this other photographer, Jesse, who can come on a little strong and I don't appreciate it. With you by my side, I think he'll leave me alone."

"Oh, he'll leave you alone," Nick said protectively.

Cass didn't let herself read anything in to the sexy alpha tone of his voice. He protected people for a living. "So, you'll do it?"

"Yeah, I'll do it." Tiny lines fanned out from the corners of his eyes like it pained him to say that. She almost told him never mind before remembering it was okay to ask for what she wanted.

"It's on the twenty-fifth. You'll still be here?"

"I'm here until around the first, so yeah." Boisterous laughs from downstairs drew Nick's attention toward the open doorway. "We should probably head down."

"Probably."

Neither of them moved.

Cassidy noticed some sandwiches on a card table in the corner and beers chilling in an ice bucket. "Or we could stay up here and avoid the awkward congratulations from everyone who may see this as more than a business transaction." She walked toward the food and drink.

"I'm on board with that plan." He grabbed two bottles of beer, shook the condensation off, and sat on the only other piece of furniture besides the table, a tan leather couch.

Cass handed him a sandwich. He handed her a beer. Their knees bumped when she sat beside him. From across the room, the couch hadn't seemed so small and narrow. The six-foot-something, broad-shouldered, muscled navy firefighter took up some space. She pretended not to notice.

And squirmed a little to find a more comfortable position so her tailbone didn't hurt quite so much.

He cleared his throat. "Can I get you a donut?"

She glanced around the room for donuts, but didn't see any. Sugary foods weren't high on her list, she was more of a salty girl, but maybe this was his way of making peace and she didn't want to be rude. "When I finish my sandwich, sure."

"Not right now?" he asked with amusement.

What was so funny? "Okay, donut man, what am I missing?"

"A donut."

She looked daggers at him.

"Not the edible kind. The kind you sit on when your rear end is still sore from falling on it."

Damn it. Her wriggle hadn't been as covert as she'd hoped. "Ha, ha, very funny. You know, if you're so concerned with the well-being of my rear end, maybe you should offer to massage it or something?"

Nick spit out his beer, luckily not in her direction, and looked to struggle with a comeback.

No worries. Cass had surprisingly more to say. Something about seeing Nick flustered brought out the flirty chatter bug in her. "Or are you afraid that would elevate my crush to lust and that I'd want to have your babies?" He choked. "Because I can save you the worry. The last man on the planet thing? That also extends to getting physical for purely sexual reasons. I'd much rather take matters into my own hands, which should tell you I have zero feelings where you're concerned."

He wiped the back of his hand across his very nice—very plain!—mouth. "You done?"

"Yes."

"Good."

They ate and drank in silence after that. Well, not exactly in silence since they could hear voices and music from downstairs. She'd eaten with the Palotay family at their kitchen table hundreds of times, but never just with Nick. Despite her new displeasure with him and his not so new annoyance with her, it felt strangely comfortable.

She didn't know him anymore. Not beyond the superficial things Rowan had shared from time to time. But one thing hadn't changed. He still considered her a pest and she still harbored secret fantasies about him. Next weekend would take care of both. She'd show him the grown-up version of herself and get him out of her system at the same time.

All while she kept her defenses in place and any disappointment a million miles away.

Chapter Four

FRIDAY MORNING CASSIDY put her weekend bag by the front door and looked out the bay window toward the *For Sale* sign, still not sure how she felt about her parents' agreement that they sell the house she grew up in. And still uncertain about which coast she'd make home now. Her good friend Julie wanted her in New York. "Roommates!" Julie had suggested. But Cass liked her independence and wasn't sure she could keep up with Julie's zero-to-sixty in three seconds mentality.

Evan wanted her to move to the west coast. He also wanted more than friendship if the one kiss they'd shared the last time she was in LA was any indication. She smiled to herself. The kiss had lasted for a good five minutes and been nothing like her previous boyfriends' kisses. But Evan had recently broken up with his longtime girlfriend and Cass didn't want to be rebound girl. Even though that might be just what she needed. She could trust Evan to be good to her for however long it lasted.

The sale sign, hanging from a wood post, swung gently in the morning breeze. Her parents wanted her to visit them in Florida next month. Retired there for the past three years, she'd made the trip twice, but that wasn't enough according to her mom. And now that Cass planned to move out of the house, they wanted her to hand deliver a few special items they hadn't taken with them.

A sporty, black SUV pulled up to the curb, squashing any more thoughts about the house. A few seconds later, Nick walked around the back of the vehicle. He had on tan cargo pants, a light blue, long-sleeved Henley that molded to his chest and arm muscles, and the same black boots he'd worn at the auction.

His gaze flicked to the window and she jumped back, hoping she hadn't been caught watching him. How ridiculous that every time he focused his deep blue regard on her, she wondered what he looked like naked. She'd had all week to prepare for this, but seeing him twice over the past six days hadn't helped to keep her mind off him.

At Rowan's insistence, Cass had joined the Palotay family for dinner the night after the auction. Nick had actually cracked a relaxed smile at something Cass said, earning him a genuine smile in return. Then on Tuesday she'd bumped into him at the supermarket—literally—when she rounded the corner of the produce section with a bag full of tomatoes, a banana, and two cucumbers. She bounced off him unscathed. He'd spilled the coffee in his hand down the front of his white T-shirt.

Cass was mortified. He'd looked ready to bawl her out,

but instead cracked up. "You're a walking, talking danger zone." He'd teased. She offered to buy him another coffee. He asked where the fire was, and then before she could answer, his attitude changed. The poking fun stopped. All signs of the charming, extrovert fled. He left with barely a good-bye.

The doorbell rang a second time.

She reminded herself Nick was a friend and this weekend was about taking a safe trip on the wild side and putting caution in a time out, nothing more.

She opened the door. "Hi."

"Hey. Sorry I'm a few minutes late. You ready to go?"

"Yep," she said, staring up at him.

He hadn't shaved. Dark stubble covered his angular jaw, chin, and upper lip. His cheeks were flushed, like maybe he'd gone for a run this morning. He also smelled shower fresh.

"Great." A lock of hair fell across his forehead as he stepped into the entryway and leaned over to pick up her bag.

They walked to his car in silence, her mind stupidly on his hair and imagining her fingers running through it. He opened the passenger door for her, tossed her bag in the back, and off they went. She'd been worried about what to talk about on the four-hour drive, but he solved that dilemma by turning on the radio the second after she clicked her seatbelt into place.

Did she say four-hour drive? Nick got them to Jackson

Hole in three and a half and took them straight to a small airport. "So skydiving is up first?" she asked.

"The weather is perfect this afternoon and my buddy Colin has time to take us up. You mentioned you were a little nervous, but excited. That still the case?"

"Yes. I'm actually more excited and less nervous now that we're here. I watched the video on the company's website so I know what to expect, which for me is key."

Nick slid his sunglasses to the top of his head and glanced at her as he pulled up to a black iron gate. She quickly turned away to look out the passenger window since she hadn't meant to reveal that particular detail. "I'm happy to run down how it's going to go from start to finish before we head inside," he said.

"I'm good, but thanks."

He reached out his window to press several numbers on a keypad. The gate slid open. "Colin's taken thousands of jumpers up. He was a Leap Frog before retiring from the navy."

"I'm not sure what that is."

"Navy parachute team."

"So if he was in the air and you were on the sea, how did you two meet?"

"We met through his brother." Nick parked near a small two-story building and hopped out of the car.

Cassidy met him around the back. "Was he in emergency, fire and rescue with you?"

Nick let out a regretful sigh. "Yeah. Alex was one of the friends I lost last month." He slipped his shades back over his eyes. "Come on. Let's get you in the sky."

"Hey," she said, putting her hand on his arm. "I'm really sorry about your friends. I've never lost someone close to me, but I imagine it takes time to get past the hurt."

"It does," he said, stepping away like he didn't want to talk about it anymore.

She understood that, so veered the conversation to something easier. "How many times have you done this?"

"I've lost count, but enough to play instructor for today."

"Wait. You mean I'm tandem jumping with you, not Colin?" She quickened her steps to keep up with Nick's long strides around the building.

"Colin's piloting. He owns the company. That's his plane there." Nick nodded to a small white airplane with a blue racing stripe down the side.

Cass had flown commercial airlines hundreds of times without a problem, but the sight of the three-wheeled propeller plane made her palms sweat. The thought of jumping out of a plane attached to Nick did, too, but for entirely different reasons.

He's a cocky jerk who thinks you're a problem.

"Colin sounds pretty awesome. Is he single?"

Nick stopped, turned to her. "You're asking about another guy while on a weekend date with me?"

"This isn't a date. It's a business transaction." She gave

him her biggest, widest unaffected smile.

"He's not your type." Nick resumed walking.

"You have no idea what my type is."

"I know it's not a guy who can drink a rugby team under the table, jumps off cliffs and bridges like it's nothing, and sleeps with women for sport."

"You—"

"And it's definitely not someone who doesn't have a prudent bone in his body." He glanced at her. "Except when he's flying customers."

Cassidy stopped walking. Nick noticed a second later that she wasn't beside him and twisted around.

"You don't know me, Nick. What might have been true twelve years ago isn't anymore, and if I don't want to move carefully, then I won't. And not you or anyone else gets a say in it."

They stared at each other for what felt like an eternity. "Fine," he finally said.

"Thank you."

He mumbled something under his breath as he turned away and took the few steps to the building's entrance. She gave him a small smile as he held the glass door open for her to enter first. The simple concrete-floored interior included racks filled with equipment and a seating area with couches and a coffee table. To her right was a reception desk with an office behind it.

A man who looked maybe five to ten years older than her

strode out of the office, bypassing the secretary at the desk. "Nicky Palotay. It's good to see you again." The man extended his hand before pulling Nick in for a one-armed hug.

"You, too. How are…" Nick's voice faltered. "How's the family doing?"

The guy frowned. "Wipe that depressing look off your pretty-boy face right now or I'm going to kick your ass."

"Yes, sir."

Cass watched the exchange between the men, fascinated by the glimpse into Nick's world outside of Marietta. She also noted Nick's face relaxed some at the order his friend gave.

"That's better. We're doing fine. Every day gets easier." The man turned his attention to Cass. "You must be Cassidy. Colin Andrews. It's nice to meet you."

"You, too." Cass shook his hand. "I'm sorry about your brother."

"Thanks. I appreciate that." Then to Nick he said, "She's a hell of a lot prettier than your last jumping partner."

"You can say that again."

It pleased Cass to hear Nick say that way more than it should. He was just agreeing with Colin to be polite. But maybe he had noticed she wasn't the same gawky kid from their youth. Not that it mattered if he looked at her differently. She wanted an adventure from him, his help to lift her wings so she could fly more freely in the future.

"You ready to get started?" Colin asked her.

"Super ready." She filled out paperwork at the reception desk and dropped the pen back in the pencil holder at the same time Nick announced it was time to gear up.

"The harness should be snug and comfortable," he said, pulling and tugging on the straps and metal fittings around her body. The back of his hands grazed her jean-clad thighs. His fingertips skimmed over her back and sides. Innocent touches that from any other man wouldn't have registered a thing. But with Nick, her body responded with vibrations from the base of her spine to the back of her neck. She pressed a few fingers to her nape to stave off the warmth there.

He continued to stand close enough that his clean, masculine scent filled her senses while he gave instructions that included what to expect, where to put her hands, and where *not* to put her hands when she jumped out of the airplane. She listened carefully, knowing no matter what, she'd feel safe because she'd be harnessed to him.

"...And if you forget everything I just said, no worries. I've got you." His eyes met hers for the first time since he'd started prepping her.

"Okay," she said softly, staring into an electric blue sea she wouldn't mind being stranded in for—she blinked, dropped her chin, and looked herself over. There was no getting marooned with Nick. Taking one of the straps in her hand she said, "Is this thing tight enough?"

"No. But I'm not finished yet." Nick stepped into his harness and pulled it up. "We'll tighten things up on the plane."

They walked outside onto the tarmac and approached the plane from the back. Colin sat in the pilot's seat, his attention on the control board. Nick climbed into the small empty cabin of the plane first, got situated with his back against the pilot's seat, his legs straight out in front of him, then gave her his hand. She linked her fingers with his. He helped guide her into his lap, her back to his front.

Nick slid the door shut, the plane roared to life. With nothing to hold on to, Cass had no other option but to sink more intimately in between Nick's legs and relax against his chest so she didn't topple over as they sped down the runway and took to the sky. Pretty much every nerve in her body fired a feel-good sensation from their cozy position.

She looked out the window during the smooth lift off, excitement of a different kind growing inside her. She'd never pictured herself skydiving and gave herself a mental high five.

"Just passing five thousand feet," Colin shouted over the loud staccato sound of the engine several minutes later.

"This is the altitude I'll be opening our chute," Nick said, voice raised. "Unless you want the honors."

"I can pull the parachute?"

"If you ask nicely."

She turned her head and almost bumped noses with him.

When she discovered a playful gleam in his eyes, she fought the urge to share an Eskimo kiss and gave him the back of her head again. "I'd love to pull the parachute please," she called out.

"You got it."

"How high up are we going?"

"Ten thousand feet. Here," he handed her the pair of goggles he'd mentioned earlier. "Put these on. We're almost there. You're going to feel me working behind you as I attach us together. Your harness will feel tighter now."

"Okay."

Cassidy admired the snow-covered mountains in the distance and a powder blue sky that stretched as far as she could see. Connectors locked into place, the sound of metal reassuring, but even if she couldn't hear anything, she had the feeling she'd still be unafraid. She had nothing to worry about with Nick at her back.

"It's time," he said, reaching over to open the door. A cold wind whirled through the plane, hitting her cheeks as Nick maneuvered them so they could make their way to the opening. She stepped out onto the small aluminum platform the size of a shoebox, looked down at the land, miles below them. Time stood still and sped up at the same time. "Ready…set… Go!" he shouted.

She stepped into the air.

The rush and roar of the wind hit her full force, her stomach left her for a second. A feeling of euphoria flooded her. *I'm flying.* Being truly weightless and falling through the air with Nick's broad chest and strong arms keeping her somewhat cocooned, she'd never been more at peace or so overwhelmed with sensations of exhilaration. He took her wrists and spread her arms wide as they continued their freefall. Adrenaline pumped through her veins, a gigantic smile took hold of her face.

"You're doing fantastic," Nick called out.

She couldn't respond. Couldn't stop grinning. She'd seen so much beauty and wonder from behind her camera lens, but getting a birds-eye view of earth like this, like she was this tiny little part of the universe in a moment in time that meant something to no one else but her, was breathtaking.

Nick took her right hand inside his and together they pulled the chute. The wind stopped. The straps around her thighs and under her arms pinched as she and Nick jerked up before slowing down considerably.

"That was incredible!" Cass closed her eyes for a moment to tuck the memory of free falling into the back of her mind for safekeeping.

"It was," Nick agreed.

"I want to do it again."

Hew chuckled. "How about for now, I let you steer?"

She slid her goggles off so they hung around her neck, let her head fall back against Nick's chest. "I'd like that." Lifting her arms and gripping the straps he guided her to, she tugged gently on the right one so they turned right. Then the left so they turned left.

She wished they could float in the sky for hours instead of minutes. Being under the canopy of their chute filled her with tranquility. She had a feeling Nick enjoyed the respite, too.

Being alone with him like this roused all sorts of emotions inside her, from gratitude to curiosity. What else could he show her? Share with her? How many other girls had he taken to new heights? These magical, special minutes were unique for her only, she knew, but maybe before the weekend ended, she'd find a way to gift him with something new, too.

WITH A MINUTE left to go before they touched ground, Nick took over steering to guide them to a safe landing. They jogged to a stop while the parachute came to a rest on the wet, green grass behind them. He unhooked the four-point harness keeping them connected and immediately missed being close to Sid when she stepped away.

Even with equipment between their bodies, he'd enjoyed the feel of her curves, the warmth being in contact with her generated. And she smelled fantastic, sweet with a hint of something fruity, more feminine than anything he'd inhaled before.

She spun around. Rosy cheeks, pink lips pulled up in an infectious smile, emerald eyes sparkling. He didn't take many pictures, but he had the urge to pull his cell phone out of his zippered pocket and capture the beauty in front of him.

"That was the best thing ever!" She lunged at him, almost knocking him off balance. "Thank you, thank you, thank you," she said, wrapping her arms around his neck. "I loved every minute of it."

He kept his arms at his side, unnerved by the way she made him think and feel things he didn't want to.

She backed away quickly as if sensing his discomfort. "Sorry. There's probably a no touching rule unless it's required, right? I just feel so…so alive." She bounced in place. "And I couldn't help myself. It won't happen again. Promise."

Her vow depressed him when it should have made him damn happy.

"No worries," he said.

"I can see how people get addicted to this. Oh, hello!" She turned her attention to their ride back to the airport, one of the local college kids Colin hired to gather the equipment and play shuttle driver. The guy introduced himself and moved to undo Sid's harness.

"I've got that," Nick said, elbowing the kid out of the way.

Five minutes later, he and Sid were in the backseat of a Jeep for the ten-mile return drive. Per usual after first jumps, the high Sid experienced came to a crashing low. She slouched against the passenger door, her eyes fluttered shut.

He allowed himself a few moments to stare at her wholesome, beautiful face before his head fell back against the seat, his gaze going out the passenger window.

Colin had done him a solid making this happen on short notice with a packed schedule. And with family obligations Nick couldn't bring himself to even imagine. If anything ever happened to Rowan, he'd lose his shit and not be nearly as hospitable as Colin. As hard as it was to accept losing Jake and Alex on the sub fire last month, it was a thousand times worse for Colin. Alex had been his youngest brother, the baby among four siblings.

Baby.

Nick flexed his legs. Jesus, after twelve years, he should be over losing Sloane. Finished with the house fire that claimed her and her parents in the middle of the night. But he remembered the fierce intensity he'd loved her with like it was yesterday. Bored with the local girls, he'd fallen hard and fast for the beauty from Bozeman. They'd been high school sweethearts, madly in love, and planning their future together. Nothing mattered more to him than Sloane, not football, not anything, once he'd found out she was pregnant.

"I think I'm going to throw up," Cassidy said, snapping him out of his thoughts. She pressed the button to roll down her window.

"It's normal to feel queasy after skydiving for the first time. Should we pull over?"

She shook her head. "Are we almost there?"

"Yes."

"I am not going to ruin this perfect adventure by being sick." She undid her seatbelt to lean forward with her elbows on her knees. "You could have warned me about this, you know."

His gut clenched at her loss of a safety belt.

"Told me to expect the euphoria to settle in my stomach like bad chicken invaded my favorite burrito."

"It will pass."

"So do kidney stones."

It wasn't polite to find that funny, but he did, and barked out a laugh. He'd laughed more with Sid in the past week than he had in a hell of a long time. She gave him the stink-eye, which only made him laugh harder.

"I'm so glad you find my discomfort amusing."

"It's not that," he managed to say. "I'm really sorry you feel sick." He slid her loose ponytail over her shoulder and rubbed her back.

Confusion marred her face, whether from his words or his gentle kneading, he didn't know. Truth be told, she had him stumped, too. He'd swear his hand had acted without a signal from his brain.

"You've grown a sense of humor," he said.

She looked away. "Sometimes you have to."

So it was a defense mechanism. What—or who—had she needed defending from? And why did it hurt that she'd used it on him? He'd made it clear where the two of them stood this weekend.

The sudden sense of being a total prick lodged an uncomfortable tightness in the back of his throat. She didn't deserve to be lumped into the same category as Mandy, or any other woman, really. He'd known Sid her whole life and could handle a friendship with her. Why he hadn't gone that route earlier he didn't know.

"Hang in there a few more minutes and I'll have a cure for you."

"Is there anything you don't know how to do?"

"Apparently, I'm not very good at giving a heads-up about motion sickness." He dropped his hand.

"That was helping," she said shyly.

He debated on whether to pretend he hadn't heard that. He didn't want to give her any wrong ideas, didn't want to be too helpful. *Shit.* So much for the no touching rule, he resumed rubbing her back. "Colin sells this juice concoction that settles stomachs. He won't tell anyone what's in it, but it works like a charm every time."

"Is there pineapple juice in it?"

"I don't know. Why?"

"That's my favorite. What's yours?"

"I'm partial to orange."

"Favorite food?"

He fidgeted, but kept his hand steady on Sid's back. "Enough with the questions, Nancy Drew."

"I loved Nancy Drew."

Nick knew that. She and Rowan had read all the books and tried numerous times to get him to be the "bad guy" in their make-believe play as detectives.

Rather than admit he remembered yet another fact about his sister's best friend, he stayed quiet. With any luck Sid would, too.

"Are we there yet?" she asked.

His mouth twitched. She combined sexy and adorable in a way he'd never experienced before. That she was teasing him while her head was between her legs proved she had spunk and didn't take herself too seriously.

The car came to a stop at the gate.

Cassidy lifted up. "Thanks," she said when he dropped his hand to the seat. She pulled her hair out of the ponytail and twisted it into a bun on top of her head. A few shorter strands fell around the smooth slope of her neck. He had the urge to press his lips there, kiss, lick, find out what she tasted like.

As soon as they were parked, she jumped out of the car, raised her face to the sun, and took a deep breath. Nick thanked their driver and headed into the office. He needed a minute to get his wayward thoughts under control. When he strode back outside, she gratefully accepted the bottle of juice he'd grabbed. "This is really good. Want to try it?" She held the glass container out to him.

He tried everything at least once. "Not bad."

Watching her wrap those full lips of hers around the bottle for another sip wasn't bad either. He looked away before he thought any harder about what they might feel like working their way around his body. New rule—no more noticing Sid's body parts.

He glanced at his watch. "Think you can handle about a half hour drive to our hotel?"

"Now that I'm no longer a skydiving virgin, I think I can handle anything." If mischief had a color it was a mix between the green of her eyes and the pink in her cheeks.

A combination he didn't know if *he* could handle.

Chapter Five

CLOTHING OPTIONAL.

Cassidy couldn't get those two little words out of her head. Up to her neck in mineral-laden hot water with Nick sitting a few feet away, they both wore bathing suits because they weren't a couple, but she wished that didn't matter. She wished she were brave enough to ditch her black one-piece simply because she had the option to.

The fading sun shone through the needles of the giant pine trees surrounding the hot-spring style whirlpool and once again she hated herself for putting her trust in the wrong guy. *It's not your fault. He's to blame.* Deep down she knew that, but it didn't make what happened to her any easier. Gullible, naïve, stupid, she'd used those descriptions and more since that night in college. If only she didn't wear the reminder on her skin it might be easier to get past. The truth was, she'd always have to cover up if she didn't want to expose the sin of her misplaced affection.

She'd come a long way, had more resilience than she'd imagined, but scars left a mark inside and out forever. It was how deep she let them run that mattered.

Right now, the last thing she should be thinking about was that horrible time. She glanced over at Nick. He had his head tipped back, his eyes closed. He was so handsome she could stare at him all day. When they'd dropped their plush hotel robes to enter the hot spring, she'd gotten an eyeful of ripped stomach muscles, wide shoulders, strong arms, and almost tripped into the water face-first.

Besides the damage to her lower back, Cass liked her body, but Nick was the picture of masculinity—virile, rugged, not a flaw to be seen. He was also charming, smart, courageous, kind.

Why she'd thought this weekend a good idea she didn't know. He didn't feel even a hint of attraction toward her, so all she was doing was torturing herself with misguided admiration. Yes, she'd stepped out of her comfort zone, but at what cost?

She leaned her head back on the edge of the small pool and willed herself to melt into the wispy steam of the mineral infused water. The hot spring boasted restorative properties, the therapeutic waters promising to heal the body and soothe the soul. *Come on water, work your magic.*

Two loud, happy voices broke into the quiet serenity. Cass straightened. Nick did, too. A couple, probably in their mid-thirties, arrived at the edge of the whirlpool, big smiles on their faces.

"Hello there," the couple said in unison.

Cass scooted closer to Nick and said, "Hi" at the same

time he said, “Hey.”

“You two lovebirds don’t mind some company do you?” the woman asked.

The whirlpools were open to everyone so it was nice of her to ask and Cass was about to correct her on the “lovebirds” when their new company disrobed and, in all their naked glory, stepped into the hot spring.

Oh. Okay. Heat that had nothing to do with the water made Cass sweat. She glanced at Nick, he glanced at her, and she could tell he was thinking the same thing. Get out of the water or stay and pretend the nudity didn’t bother them?

It wasn’t the couple’s bareness that troubled Cassidy, though. She didn’t have to look at it with the water covering them up. It was that her mind immediately hurried to Nick’s naked torso and what he might look like without his trunks. What he’d feel like in her hand, in her mouth, buried deep inside her.

She looked at the bubbles swirling around them, wrapped her fingers around the edge of the seat.

“I’m Lacey and this is Ian.”

“Cassidy.”

“Nick.”

“Nice to meet you both,” Lacey said before she giggled and gave Ian a playful nudge with her shoulder. “Watch it, mister, we have company.”

Great. Ian obviously had wandering hands. Which made Cass think about Nick’s strong, capable hands straying to her body underneath the water. Her nipples pebbled.

"When has that ever bothered you?" Ian said.

This was sooo no longer a good idea. Cassidy quickly spun over to Nick so she faced him, arms straight out on either side of his body. Her fingers gripped the edge of the whirlpool. She didn't want Lacy or Ian to see her unsettled expression, but more than that, she had the urge to speak privately with Nick and not embarrass herself in front of strangers. "I think that's our cue to go," she whispered.

"I told you she didn't look the type," Lacy said, just loud enough for Cass to overhear her. It wasn't said with ill will, but stung all the same.

Cass had heard those exact same words before, from girls who judged her conservative clothes and straitlaced inclination, and guys who ignored her when she didn't indulge in careless activities with them.

Nick's eyes burned into hers, saying something very different than the words he'd used the night of the bachelor auction. They said she *was* the right type. That the couple across the way didn't know her. She shouldn't let their words bother her.

Unthinking, she moved a little closer, her thighs touching his knees under the water.

On photo shoots with her camera around her neck, situations like this never arose. She was great at her job, comfortable in the role of photographer so much so that she'd set the standard high for herself. And reached each goal she set. Impressed the people she worked with time and time again. But her perfectionism at work led to disappointment in her personal life because she still hadn't figured out how to be just a girl.

She stared at Nick. Maybe it was because she felt safer with him beside her or maybe it was because she finally had the courage to speak up, but whichever it was, she pushed off the edge and turn around.

"What type would that be?" Cass asked.

"Sid," Nick said under his breath.

"The type that has fun," Lacey said nicely. "No offense. Ian just thought you two might be up for..."

"What?" They weren't implying—

"Simultaneous orgasms," Lacey said as Ian brought her into his lap, her back to his front, his hands cupping her breasts. Breasts she had partially on display above the water line. "There's something thrilling about having someone watch," she added. "And Nick looks like someone I'd definitely like to watch me. Ian would barely have to work for it."

Nick cleared his throat. "As nice an offer as that is, Cassidy and I have plans back at our suite." He wrapped his arms around her waist and pulled her close. "Right, baby?"

Cass had no response. She couldn't form a coherent thought. Not with her body against Nick's and him whispering *baby* in her ear. And not with her completely turned on at the idea of Nick getting her off in front of this couple.

There were more than minerals swirling in this water.

And quite possibly she'd entered a dream state when she'd stepped into the whirlpool. Or maybe she *had* fallen in face first and hit her head and this was a hallucination.

"That's too bad," Lacey said. "Guess I'll just close my eyes and picture it."

Nope. Not a vision. Because, hell no. Cass didn't want Loose Lacey thinking about Nick, picturing Nick, or remembering Nick. "He's off limits," Cass said, surprised by the strength and possessive tone of her voice.

"All the better."

"That's not very nice," Cassidy said.

Lacey cocked her head to the side and looked around Cass to Nick. "I don't think he minds."

"Actually, I do. I also mind when someone makes my girl uncomfortable so we're going to leave you to it." He climbed out of the hot spring, grabbed Cassidy's robe, and then extended his hand to her. She quickly covered up. He did the same.

"Well, then, have a good night," the couple said amiably.

Nick took Cassidy's hand. "It's going to be better than good."

Cassidy flashed a smile she didn't exactly feel and hoped didn't look fake. She'd no doubt come up with the perfect parting shot in ten minutes. Keeping up with Nick's brisk pace, though, she was happy to leave her hand in his for as long as he wanted to hold it. No guy had ever defended her like that before. No guy had ever made her entire body tingle like he did. He didn't mean any of the things he'd said, but she'd pretend for a little while longer that he'd spoken the truth.

They strode through the glass doors of the gorgeous five-star hotel—that obviously catered to all sorts—their bare feet slapping against the cold, marble floor. Nick seemed determined to get them far away from the pool and the kinky couple as quickly as possible. He dropped her hand when they reached the elevators, placed his palm on the small of her back when the doors opened, and ushered her inside the empty lift.

The elevator doors closed. Cassidy looked at Nick. He looked at her. The air rippled with amusement and they both burst into laughter. Her belly laughs made her eyes tear up. "I can't believe that just happened," she said half-giggling.

Nick shrugged with a raise of his brows, intimating he'd experienced far more forward advances than a little voyeurism. Of course he had. Look at the man. Add in his firefighting military background and women no doubt offered all kinds of propositions. "I'm sorry for getting a little personal there, but I thought that was the best way to handle the situation."

"I didn't mind." From the pained look on Nick's face, though, *he* did. "I mean, I appreciated that you stuck up for us and got the last word in. Do you think they routinely hit on other couples like that and are successful?"

"Probably."

"Think they score more often than not?"

"I think it's time we change the subject."

"Why? Afraid I'll want the 4-1-1 on your sexual escapades?" She couldn't believe she'd just said that.

He stepped toe-to-toe with her before she had time to blink, his warm, strong body tantalizingly close. She swallowed the nerves clogging her throat and tilted her head back to look up at him.

"Right now, Sid? I'm afraid of you." The elevator chimed and the doors opened behind him. "So stop talking before I do something we'll both regret."

What did that mean, she wanted to ask, but he'd given her his back and already started down the hallway. She hurried through the closing elevator doors to keep up with him. There wasn't a thing he could do to her that she'd regret. Which only made their circumstances worse. It didn't matter if they had a good time together, he would never see her as anything but a nuisance.

And she couldn't stop seeing him as wonderful.

NICK POLISHED OFF his beer with a light brown-haired beauty sitting across from him on the patio of their suite. He didn't know when Sid had gone from sweet to sexy, but she had, and he didn't like it. Strike that. He knew the when—

the second he'd laid eyes on her at the river. It was the *what* that pissed him off. What an idiot he was to think she wouldn't get to him.

If anything happened between them this weekend, he'd hate himself because it would just be hooking up, and Sid wasn't wired that way. Add in her childhood crush and it made him a jackass to even think about taking advantage of their weekend away. The last thing Nick wanted was a relationship of any sort. His only agenda was to figure out what to do with the rest of his life. He'd gotten a call from the NIFC yesterday. The fire center wanted him on their management team, which meant he wouldn't necessarily be smack dab in the middle of wildland fires, but he still hadn't worked through his feelings on where his skills and training would be most beneficial, or if he should go in a totally different direction. Like lifeguarding. He closed his eyes and pictured himself on a beach in San Diego. Sand. Surf. Nothing else. The image stayed with him until Sid interrupted with, "Want to order room service for dinner?"

Since he hadn't made specific plans for tonight's meal he said, "Sure."

"It's a habit of mine," she said, standing. "When I travel for work, I tend to stay in at night. It's easier, safer, more comfortable. I could write a guide on the best room service in America," she said casually over her shoulder.

There was something not so casual in her words, though. Every little thing she shared with him made him more interested. He hadn't thought about her over the years, except for hearing occasional updates from Rowan, but being with her now, he wouldn't mind a few details. Sometime over the last week, she'd gotten under his skin and taken up space in his head. It felt good thinking about her rather than him.

He watched her walk into the living area and pick up the hotel menu. Staying in the same suite hadn't been the smartest idea. Yeah, it had two bedrooms, with enough space that they could avoid each other, but when Sid had raved about the view of the mountains and asked him to join her on the patio, he couldn't say no. She had no idea being close to her, smelling her feminine scent, and being on the receiving end of her innocent touches, was killing him.

"Safer than fighting off guys in bars and restaurants?" he asked when she sat back down to peruse the menu.

She looked at him under long, dark lashes. "Something like that." With the sun sinking behind the Teton Mountains, gold tones highlighted her natural beauty. "So, what are you in the mood for?"

You.

"Hey, they've got something called Chow Fun. I don't care what it is, I'm getting it." She ran her finger along the page as she read, "Rice noodles, mushrooms, bean sprouts, bok choy, scallions, cashews, ginger. Luckily, it sounds good." She closed the menu and handed it to him. "Here you go."

"You are fun, you know. You don't need to eat it to be it."

She chuckled. "Ha! Tell that to Loose Lacey."

"I'm telling you. I had fun today in no small part because of you." Sharing like that caused problems for a guy, but apparently Sid was a problem he wanted to keep.

"I had fun, too," she said softly before fixing her gaze on the vanishing sun. "But I think you already knew that."

He did, but it was nice to hear his auction date was a success so far. He hadn't been on a real date in years, preferring mutually satisfying hookups instead. The thought of getting close enough to a woman to feel anything more than respect and a good time put an uncomfortable knot in his stomach. Sloane had been *the* girl for him. Should he be past it? Yes. Was he? Considering he'd yet to get serious with anyone else, apparently not. How could he when doubts about keeping those he cared about safe still plagued him.

"I'll call in our order. Be right back." He decided on glazed pork chops while dialing up room service. When the man on the other end of the line asked if they'd like anything for dessert, Nick ordered the fresh berries, remembering that Sid didn't have much of a sweet tooth.

"It'll be about thirty minutes," he said, landing back on the patio. He handed Sid the blanket that had been draped over the couch. Despite the outdoor heater, the setting sun meant a rapid drop in temperature.

"Thank you." She wrapped herself in the cotton blend.

Good thing. The black leggings and cream-colored sweater were distracting when paired with her perfect curves.

Several tall, glass hurricanes with crimson candles sat on the square table between the cushioned loveseats and he remembered seeing a box of matches in the small kitchen. He went to grab them, thinking to offer light since the hurricanes supplied the only source on the patio.

Sid's attention had strayed toward the darkening sky, her profile a prettier sight than anything beyond the railing. He stared for a moment, pulled a match out. Before he could strike it, though, she grabbed his wrist with a tight grip. He dropped the stick.

"No! That's okay." She quickly let go of him, her elbow digging into her side as she pulled her arm back.

"Sid?" He'd been on enough rescue assignments to know when someone sounded scared and she'd just flipped out over candles?

"Sorry. I didn't mean to get so uptight. The ambient light coming from inside the suite is fine."

"I don't think that was uptight."

"Oh." She released a breath. "Okay. Good."

"More like panicked. What's up?" He'd never once asked her that and should have kept his mouth shut by the look of consideration on her face.

But he found himself genuinely wanting to know what made her tick. After skydiving, he knew she had an adventurous streak that had only scratched the surface. He'd noticed she fussed with her hair on long car drives, like she needed something to do with her hands. And in the hot springs he'd discovered she was protective of him, even though he didn't need protecting.

"Nothing's up."

"That was not nothing." He put the matchbox down on the table, noting she tracked his movement. Only when he'd sat back with his hands on his thighs did her shoulders relax.

"What did you order for dinner?" she said.

"Nice try."

"You ordered nice try?"

He understood not wanting to talk about things, but that only applied to him. His dad once told him if there was something he really wanted to know, a silent stare went a long way to conveying care and stubbornness at the same time, so that's what he did now.

To his surprise, Sid stared right back, held his gaze like she had no plans to back down. It made him hot. His interest climbed. No woman had ever presented such a dichotomy between vulnerability and confidence before.

"It's nothing," she said again.

"Sometimes nothing is everything."

"And you're an expert on that?"

He shrugged. "I've done my share of hiding." Still did. There were days it choked him.

She eyed him carefully. "Okay, how about we trade information then?"

Shit. He'd walked right into that. However, the fact that she made it sound about as impersonal as possible stung more than the bonehead maneuver. His own fault, given he termed what they were doing a business transaction.

"Okay. You start."

She tightened the blanket around her lap. "I don't like candles or anything with a small flame, but mostly I don't like matches."

Telling a firefighter she didn't like matches immediately sent up red flags. "You've had a bad experience with them?" Indirectly, directly, both held weight.

"Yes," she answered, jaw tight.

He let that hang between them for a minute. Rowan hadn't mentioned any fire-related incidences, but maybe whatever this was, Sid hadn't shared it with anyone. If he were smart, he'd drop the conversation right here.

"Recently?" he asked. *Dumbass.*

She chewed her bottom lip. "In college."

Nick nodded as every muscle in his body clenched. A lot of bad happened in college. Rowan had called him countless times to complain about the guys at school who only wanted in her pants and pulled stupid pranks on each other to get a girl's attention.

"So now that you know my deep, dark secret from college, tell me what keeps you up at night."

He didn't know shit about her secret, but decided to let her off the hook for as much his sake as hers.

"And don't worry about holding back. Let it all out. I know you want to, and I promise I won't tell anyone." Her cheeky smile didn't hide the warmth and genuine affection only two people who had known each other for a long time could feel. And the thing of it was, he did want her to know him. Maybe if he got a few things off his chest, he'd be able to let them go.

That had to be the reason he dropped his defenses and shared the God's honest truth. "Sloane was pregnant."

"*What?*"

"I've never told another soul that." Mostly because nobody had ever asked about him the way Sid just had.

"Wait. Your high school girlfriend, Sloane?"

He rubbed his hands down his jeans. "Yeah."

"Oh, my God." She scrambled to sit taller. "I'm so sorry. I know how hard it was for you to lose her and that's why you chose to join the navy and become a firefighter. How far along was she?"

"Twelve weeks."

"Nobody else knew?" Sid's soft voice drew his attention away from the tiled ground.

"No. We were going to tell our families that weekend. I was going to ask her to marry me. We had everything planned. Live together at college. Work my ass off playing football in hopes of making the pros." Every dream he'd had died with Sloane the night old aluminum wiring started an electrical fire that engulfed her house in a matter of minutes.

Cassidy stood, the blanket fell to the ground and, looking like an angel sent only for him, she erased the short distance between them to lean down and kiss his cheek. "I'm sorry for your loss," she whispered. "You would have been a great dad."

He put his hands on her hips to stop her withdraw. That was exactly what he'd needed to hear after all this time. He'd needed someone to erase his doubts so he could live with what might have been and stow it away in a memory box.

She peered down at him, a mix of surprise and regard on her face. They stayed like that, stock still, until she sat next to him, took his hand in hers, and laid her head on his shoulder. The loveseat didn't allow for any space between them so their clasped hands sat atop his thigh. Heat stroked between his legs.

"I've never lost someone I love, but I imagine it's unbearable and not easy to talk about." Her thumb rubbed over his knuckles. "Sloane was lucky, though. She got to experience love before she passed away. And I have a feeling she's looking down on you and very proud of the man you've become."

Nick turned his head to say thanks at the same time Sid lifted hers to look up at him. Their lips were mere inches from each other. Her gaze dropped to his mouth. A split second later, said mouth was on hers.

In thanks. In surrender. Hell, he didn't know what he was doing.

She pulled back, caught her breath. Damn it. He'd screwed up.

Or not.

Because she placed her hands on his shoulders and straddled his lap. With her intense green eyes melting into his, she canted her head closer. Anticipation made him slide his palms up her back. His fingers ran through the long, loose strands of her hair. *Take what you want, Sid, before we remember this isn't a good idea.*

She tilted her head to the right. He went left. And their lips collided again. With fire, passion, *need.* She was the first person to climb over the wall around his heart and he wanted to celebrate it exactly this way.

He moved his hands to her nape, swore he could feel her pulse on his skin, her heart beating as fast as his. She changed the tempo, kissed him softly, in the middle of his mouth, the corners, back to the middle. He went along for whatever ride she wanted to take him on because if he took charge she'd be naked in under a minute. And as good as that sounded, he still had enough willpower and common sense to know that would be a big mistake.

Damn, but he'd never been kissed with so much tenderness before. It kind of wrecked him. He didn't want to be treated with sweet gloves. A hold like that did damage—to both parties. He'd rather she be indifferent.

Not going to happen with Sid, you idiot.

Adding insult to injury, she dropped fluttery kisses along

his jaw and worked her way to his neck. Helpless against this feel-good assault, he lifted his chin as she parted her lips to fire openmouthed kisses just below his ear that were so damn hot an actual shiver raced down his spine.

What the hell was this girl doing to him?

A loud knock sounded on the hotel room door. She startled and broke contact. He let out a small groan at the interruption.

"Oh, my God," she said, and scrambled to her feet. It took her a good long second to get her balance. Once steady, she ran the pads of her fingers across her bottom lip. "I'm sor—" She shook her head. "I'll get the door."

He watched her hurry away, not sorry either, but it was for the best that they'd stopped. Besides their misaligned feelings for one another, she had a thriving career and plans to move to New York or LA. He was trying to figure his future out, and most likely off to Idaho at the beginning of next the month. Cassidy was the kind of girl who formed relationships and kept them, but they had no chance at a future together.

No good reason to pick up where they'd left off without her getting hurt.

Chapter Six

THE WIRES WERE crossed in Cassidy's brain. That was the only explanation she had for consoling Nick by straddling and kissing him last night. For telling him she hated matches. For liking on him harder because he'd actually opened up to her.

And then pretended as if none of it had happened.

He'd simply slid right past all those biggies when dinner arrived and treated her like a kid sister again, going so far as to tell her she was grumpy if she didn't get enough sleep so they'd better turn in early since they had a date at dawn with a wildlife tour.

She planned to give him grumpy and then some this morning.

Not a hard task considering they were currently zipping along rugged terrain in an open-air four-wheel drive Jeep in search of elk, moose, bears, wolves, eagles and more, according to their too-happy-for-this-early-in-the-morning naturalist guide. And by zipping she meant she wished she'd brought a pillow to sit on. Her tailbone still liked to complain when put in touch with less than gentle circumstances.

The Jeep hit a particularly rough patch. She tried not to wince.

Nick chuckled, the jerkwad. He seemed to be in an awfully good mood this morning. His shoulder brushed hers as he said, "Sorry about all the bumps."

"I'm a little disappointed you didn't put in for a smooth ride."

"Sometimes difficult is better. More fun."

She glared at him. "Do not go tossing the F word at me before I've had my coffee."

He laughed again. The sound made her less grumpy, damn him.

Time to focus on their adventure. She stared out toward the unobstructed view of the national park. The mountain landscape with towering jagged snow-covered peaks looked ethereal. Hundreds of miles of trails surrounded them in beautiful earth tones.

She tightened the scarf around her neck and tugged her black knit cap more fully over her ears to stave off the cold wind hitting her cheeks. Her eyes watered, but she much preferred the open-air vehicle to something enclosed. With the sky growing a deeper blue as the sun rose higher, she'd always remember this early morning escapade.

With Nick.

The Jeep slowed to a stop. While their guide spoke on the geology and ecology of the park, Nick pulled a long, silver cylinder out from underneath the seat. Two paper cups materialized next. "Coffee?"

No matter how hard she pressed her lips together, she couldn't stop her smile. "Yes, please."

He poured them each a cup.

"Grizzly bear three o'clock," their guide said.

Coffee sloshed out of Cassidy's cup as she whipped around for a look. She'd traveled to dozens of special places and taken pictures of hundreds of people, but she'd never been this close to wild animals before. *There he is.* She put her drink down near her feet, picked up the provided binoculars.

"He's beautiful," she muttered.

"He's huge," Nick said over her shoulder.

"I wish I had my camera with me." Why had she let Rowan talk her out of bringing it? Oh yeah, because Ro had threatened to put her on *two* dating websites if she didn't enjoy her bachelor-buy without the safety net of her Nikon.

Out of the corner of her eye, she caught Nick passing her something. She lowered the binoculars reluctantly, hating to miss a second with Mr. Grizzly. "What's this?"

"It's one of those disposable cameras. I know it won't take near the pictures you normally capture, but at least you'll have something on film to remember today by."

She took the piece of rubbish thinking *this is the best gift anyone's ever given me.* That Nick thought to snag the unnecessary device—they had their cell phones—meant he was thinking about her whether he wanted to or not.

She leaned over and kissed him. Nothing serious. Just a quick peck on the mouth. "That was really thoughtful. I love it."

He might regret sharing secrets last night, but she knew he didn't regret the kisses she'd given him. She'd heard the little hum in the back of his throat when she'd kissed his neck with her lips and tongue. So she didn't see any harm in doing something he liked again in thanks.

Plus, she loved catching him off guard and by the stunned look on his face she'd succeeded. *That's right, Nick Palotay, this girl is all about living without apology.*

"I'm glad," he said.

"I'm glad you're glad."

"I think the bear is glad, too. He's coming closer."

She twisted around. "Holy Yogi Bear, he is." She ran her thumb over the thingamajig that clicked the film to the right position before lifting it to her face. The bear needed to get really close if she wanted to capture any details, but even if he turned out to look like a black blob, she'd love the picture.

"Look up," Nick said.

An eagle soared right above them. She snapped a photo, inwardly laughing because she *maybe* got the tip of its wing.

Their guide started up the engine again. He took the next several miles at a slower pace because it seemed a switch had been turned on their safari and all the animals came out to say hello. Cass used the binoculars, took more photos sure to be grainy but wonderful, slipped into easy conversation with Nick.

"I'm telling you it's a donkey, not a dog," he said.

"We are so googling animal crackers when we get back to the hotel." She hadn't eaten the snack in a long time, but she did not remember a donkey. "There is definitely a dog."

"No dog."

"I'll bet you there's a dog."

"You're on," he said, all smug and annoying. "What do I get when I win?"

"Other way around, Palotay." Cass gripped the roll bar to keep from jostling into Nick's side every five seconds as they traveled over another rough patch of ground.

Nick smiled at her like he knew he had this in the bag then looked away. "Looks like you had a fire not too long ago," he called to their driver and guide.

Cassidy noted the charred ground and burnt trees in the distance.

"Happened last year."

"I hope no animals or people were injured," Nick said.

"Thankfully, no."

He smiled to himself at that, but Cass caught it. Her stupid heart did, too. How was she supposed to stay grumpy and immune to him when he said stuff like that and did nice things like bring her coffee and buy her disposable cameras?

But then she remembered tossing and turning in bed last night, hurt by his easy dismissal of their kiss. She hadn't meant for it to happen, but some irresistible force, combined with his acquiescence, had shattered any uncertainty. Nick had a way of making her act on instinct, which was dangerous. He might have laid himself bare to her, but she'd be naïve to think it meant anything more than a passing connection.

And that was why she'd best get over her attraction to him before she engaged her heart any further. "Rowan mentioned you're taking a job with the National Interagency Fire Center."

"Haven't told them yes yet."

"Why not?"

He turned his head to look at her. "Want to be sure."

"Have you made a list of pros and cons?" She'd started two lists—one for New York and one for LA. So far they were tied.

His sexy lips curved. "Lists really aren't my thing, but I bet you keep meticulous track of things."

How did he know that? Was she that obviously organized with her life? Because there were actually plenty of days when she felt out of her element. Hence why she kept a pad of paper and sticky notes everywhere.

"Yeah, you keep lists," he said, dipping his head to look her right in the eyes when she didn't answer right away.

"You say that like there's something wrong with them."

"Not at all." He lifted his hands up in innocent retreat.

"But?"

"No buts." He grabbed the roll bar when the Jeep traveled over a bump in the dirt road.

She made an annoyed face at him.

"Okay, I'm doubtful that they really do any good. I mean just because you write something down doesn't mean it will do any good."

"You've never written yourself a reminder note?" If he said no she'd have to push him out of the jeep because, come on, he couldn't be that perfect.

"That's different. It's a note."

"What's the last note you wrote?" A note and list was often pretty much the same thing.

He glanced over her shoulder. "Pick up Cassidy Friday at eight AM."

The insinuation that he couldn't remember to pick her up for their weekend hurt more than she cared to admit. She masked her disappointment with a blank expression and said, "I rest my case."

"I don't think—"

"Oh! Bison nine o'clock," she interrupted. Nick kept his attention on her for a beat longer before he turned around to check out the small group of buffalo. He brushed his fingers through his hair to move the strands off his forehead.

For the rest of the tour they stayed quiet, letting their tour guide do all of the talking. At one point her lack of sleep caught up with her. She leaned against Nick's side, closed her eyes for a few minutes.

When they arrived back at their departure point she thanked their guide. Then she wrapped her arms around Nick, put her mouth to his ear and said, "That was really fantastic. Thank you."

"I aim to please on this weekend getaway."

"You're doing a great job." She pulled back and watched as he thanked their driver and handed him a tip.

The minute they got in Nick's car for the drive back to the hotel, he turned to her. "The note. To pick you up? There was more to it. I'd also written 'don't be late' and that was the important part because I'm late everywhere I go and I didn't want to be late picking you up. So it wasn't a reminder. It was a kick in the ass to show up early for a change."

"You were a few minutes late," she said, secretly delighted by his clarification.

"Yeah." He smiled. "I rest my case."

She laughed and settled back in her seat. "Okay, then."

He started the car. "Glad we're on the same page."

"Are we?" She rolled her head to the side to peer at him. She was pretty sure if they compared the passages in their heads there would be few similarities.

"Maybe for this weekend we should be," he said, his eyes on the road as he hit the gas.

Her stomach dipped at his unexpected proposition. Perhaps he wasn't so unaffected by their kiss last night. "Maybe we should." She didn't know if she could trust herself to take what he offered and leave it at that, but miles away from their normal lives, why not have what she wanted? It was time Cassidy Ware added some fun, new, impulsive pages to her story.

Even if they ended up burning her.

AFTER THE WHOLE candle and match thing, Nick had changed their dinner reservation for tonight. Romantic hadn't been his angle, but when he'd inquired with the concierge about the restaurant and been told that yes, there were candles on every table, he'd asked for another recommendation. The concierge had practically jumped up and down with excitement and mentioned dining in the dark. The fixed menu is amazing and the experience one of a kind, she'd said. Since he wasn't too picky, he agreed with her suggestion. She booked them a table at seven o'clock. He got directions, said thanks, and walked away. "It's very romantic," she called after him. "Enjoy!"

He and Sid now stood at the front desk of Ebony, a chic, upscale restaurant where customers dined in complete darkness. He'd heard the concierge say dark, but he'd pictured low, moderate lighting, nothing like this.

The hostess led them to a table with a tiny flashlight in her hand. Sid slipped into the small round booth first. He followed right behind, their hands brushing on the leather seat as he overshot the distance between them. "Your waiter will be right with you," the hostess said, plunging them in total blackness as she turned to go sans light.

Sid giggled. "I can tell by the look on your face—I mean I *could* tell a minute ago that this isn't what you were expecting."

"No, it's not. You okay with it?"

"I'm good. This is the perfect date restaurant, you know. Not that we're on a date. It's just that now I don't have to worry about food stuck in my teeth or get embarrassed if I spill something on my sweater."

A sweater he liked a lot with a deep V-neck that allowed a glimpse of her black lace bra when she moved a certain way. Not that he was fixated on her chest or anything. Too bad his imagination would be the only thing on duty tonight, though, since he couldn't even see his hand when he lifted it in front of his face.

"Good evening," a man said, startling both of them. Nick knew this because Sid made a squeaking sound.

"Hi," Sid said.

"I'm Derek. I'll be your server for tonight. Welcome to Ebony. Is this your first time dining with us?"

"Yes," Nick and Sid said.

"Great. A little about tonight, then. Our philosophy here is that without visual stimulation, the pitch black heightens your other senses. You can only feel, taste, and smell."

"And hear," Sid piped in.

Derek chuckled. "Right. But we frown on loud chewing

and hope you'll keep your conversation quiet so as not to bother our other customers. We want dinner to be about experiencing the food and each other in a unique and sensual way."

They weren't touching, but Nick could swear Sid shivered.

"In other words, feel free to enjoy the meal however you'd like," Derek continued. "But if you prefer to play it safe, there is silverware on the table. What can I get you two to drink?"

"Just water please," Sid said.

Nick wanted a shot—or three—but went with Sid's choice. "Same here."

"I'll be back with your waters and first course."

"I wonder what he looks like," Sid whispered, leaning close enough for her breath to fan across his cheek. "He has a nice voice."

Two things struck Nick. One, he didn't like that she'd noticed their waiter's voice enough to wonder about him. And two, he wanted to feel her breath ghost along other parts of his anatomy.

Pushing those thoughts aside, he felt around the tabletop, finding a large round plate, eating utensils, cloth napkin, and Sid's hand.

"Oops. Sorry," she said. "I was trying to find my place setting."

"I have a feeling we'll be bumping into each other a lot,

so don't sweat it."

"Is that your way of saying you plan to eat off my plate, because I don't share with just anyone."

He grinned. "What's a guy have to do to rank sharing your meal?"

"In this situation, nothing. I won't know if you take my food or not," she said easily. Her elbow bumped his side. "Ack. Sorry. I should scoot over."

"Don't." He wrapped his arm around her shoulders. "I said don't worry about it. We're supposed to be close to get the full experience here."

She relaxed against his side. "Okay. But I should warn you. I like to eat off other people's plates, too."

"With the right incentive, I can be persuaded to share." Her hair tickled his nose. It smelled like pink grapefruit.

"I'm pretty sure this is going to be a free for all, unless you want to take the civilized route," she said.

"Civilized?"

"We move apart and use our forks and knives. Put our napkins on our laps. I think we've eaten enough meals to go through the motions of eating properly even if we can't see anything."

"And uncivilized?"

"I stay right where I am and we don't follow the rules or good manners. Just do what we want as Derek suggested. I'm not afraid to get messy, are you?"

Things had already gotten messy. And they were about

to get worse. With her warm body nestled against his, her sexy voice, and kind, intelligent disposition, he was all in to get messy, get distracted, get naked… "Not at all."

"Your first course," Derek announced. "Truffle Mortadella. Cured pork sausage in a black truffle sauce." Derek must have a lot of practice working here because Nick heard a plate land on top of the one in front of him without a hitch. "Water glasses are at eleven o'clock," their waiter added.

"It's a good thing I'm not wearing white," Sid said, laughter in her voice, and he admired her spunk even more. "Okay, first bite goes to you for bringing me on an adventure this weekend."

Sid's aim was perfect as she pressed a piece of sausage to his lips. The round piece of meat was warm, the scent sweet and spicy. He opened his mouth and her fingers grazed his lips as she placed the bite on his tongue.

Nick had been in plenty of work situations where there was almost zero percent visibility and his other senses had had to kick in. Where adrenaline and strength played a big part in his body's response. But being with Sid like this, her body heat mingling with his, her hands feeding him, the two of them unable to see a thing, stirred a reaction he hadn't felt in forever. She had him forgetting everything but being in the moment.

She made a sucking sound like she'd licked her fingers of the truffle oil. "Mmm. That's really good."

He reached out and picked up a piece of sausage. Warm and wet with sauce, a bit of the liquid dripped down his finger. "It is," he said, finished chewing. "Now it's your turn." His hand hovered for a moment until she slid her palm down his arm to his wrist and helped guide him to her mouth.

When he tried to pull his arm back, she held tight while she chewed and swallowed. "That was yummy, but I bet this is better." She brought his hand back to her mouth. Using her free hand as a guide, she gently grasped the base of his fingers and found the tip of his pointer finger with her tongue. Then she slid the whole digit into her mouth and licked it clean. Did the same to his thumb.

Aw, hell. What little restraint he had left snapped as her sucking hit him right behind his zipper. Twice now she'd put her mouth on him, rolled her tongue over his skin, and he wanted to return the favor on all her pleasure points. But she had to know this couldn't lead to anything more before they went further.

"I was right," she said, releasing him.

"Sid."

"Do not give me a speech about how you don't want me to get the wrong idea. I have lots of good ideas, Nick, and they all center on tonight. Nothing more."

How was a guy supposed to say no to that?

"Perfect," he said right before he cupped her jaw and without warning, kissed her.

He wasn't gentle. He claimed her mouth so she would know it belonged to him and he wanted this as much as she did. *No doubts, Sid.* This wasn't something that didn't matter, that wouldn't leave a mark on him, too. He kissed her with all the pent-up desire he'd barely kept under control since last night.

Her lips were soft, warm, pliant. They tasted like the truffle sauce. She sighed when he parted them to tangle his tongue with hers. Hearing her pleasure made him want to hear all her sounds, but mostly the ones she'd make when he licked and sucked on her nipples and between her legs. Actually, there wasn't a part of her he wanted to leave untouched. Mapping her body with his hands and mouth would be *his* pleasure.

The kiss exploded after that. She fisted his shirt in her hands, kissed him back with the kind of raw, hot urgency that would have brought him to his knees if he were standing. He'd never been kissed with such wild abandon. Maybe it was the dark. Or maybe it was a peek at what he could expect with Sid.

"Jesus." He heard himself growl. She murmured something in response he couldn't decode, probably because she'd knocked him senseless, and then she slowly pulled back.

He wished he could see her face.

"That was nice," she said breathlessly.

"Nice?" He shot back, equally out of breath. And he was so hard it bordered on painful.

"Super nice?"

She was messing with him. He could hear the goad in her voice. Accustomed to their nearness and personal space now, he palmed the back of her head and took her bottom lip between his teeth. "Careful, Sid, I can play right back."

"I want you to." To prove her point, she nipped him in return.

His dick got even harder. He liked this uninhibited side of Sid. He liked it a lot.

"Should we finish our Truffle Mortadella?" he asked. *Before I strip you naked right here.*

"We should. I'm really hungry."

They fed themselves and fed each other. The bites Sid gave him tasted infinitely better than the ones he took for himself because the pads of her fingers lingered on his lips for an extra second.

"Do you ever miss playing football?" she asked while they waited for their main course. She had his hand in her much smaller one, drew lazy circles on his palm with her fingernail.

The question, out of left field, caught him unaware. He normally would have brushed it off and changed the subject, but her touch combined with her kindhearted voice had him willing to answer.

"Sometimes. Not as much as I used to." He didn't miss anything as much as he used to. Time had a way of helping with that.

"If you could go back and change one thing about—"

She dropped his hand. "I'm sorry. Forget I said that. That was really insensitive and—"

"It's okay."

"Jumbo prawns simmered with tomatoes and snow peas, finished with cilantro in a green curry sauce and served over jasmine rice," Derek said, the sound of plates being set down reaching Nick's ears. Perfect timing.

"It smells amazing," Sid said. "Thank you."

Nick put his arm across her body to keep her arms at her sides. "You get first taste this time."

"Okay."

He picked up a prawn, blew on it, and brought it to her mouth. "Take a bite," he said. "I'll eat the other half."

She did as he asked, moaning her approval. Then, shrouded in darkness that gave them license to go past their barriers, they ate with their hands, laughed, touched often, and reluctantly picked up their forks to use on the rice.

"Here," she said, sliding a snow pea across the seam of his lips before slipping it into his mouth. As he chewed, she giggled. "Ahh! I just dropped one into my sweater."

"I'll get it." He placed his hand on the front of her neck, then moved one finger smoothly down the center of her chest until he got to the edge of her V-neck. She sucked in a breath. He felt it at the base of his spine. "This okay?" he asked, doing the gentlemanly thing when he felt anything but. He wanted to get her off in this booth, push her somewhere she might not want to go but he knew would make her feel good.

"Yes," she whispered.

He had no idea where the snow pea went and didn't care as he played with the lace border of her bra before dipping his hand inside the lingerie to cup her breast. "You feel amazing, Sid. Soft. Full." He kneaded, fondled, ran his thumb across the stiff peak. "Insanely beautiful."

She wiggled, her knee bumped his underneath the table, and he knew instinctively that she'd spread her legs in order to touch herself.

"Where are your hands, Sid?"

"One is here." She put her palm on his thigh. "And the other is…is in my pants."

"That is hot as fuck," he whispered, pinching her nipple. "I wish I could see it." His blood hammered in his veins. He hadn't been this turned on since…since forever.

Her hand pressed into his leg. He sensed her hips lifting off the seat slightly. "Not sure I'd be doing it if you could."

"We need to get out of here." Before she dipped that hand into her underwear. *He* wanted to give her an orgasm. And he needed to do it back at their hotel because he had no plans to stop at one. There would be no sleeping for either of them tonight.

"That's a great idea. But I've been so turned on since you kissed me, that I need to take the edge off."

"No," he said hoarsely, slipping his hand out of her bra. With his other hand he gripped her forearm and tugged her hand out of her pants. “Stay on that ledge a little longer and I promise I’ll make it worth the wait.”

“Hmmmm,” she said and proceeded to tiptoe her fingers up his thigh to the hard, aching bulge in his jeans. “Since it appears you’re there with me, okay.”

That innocent enough touch to his hard-on had him shouting, “Check!” and hoping Derek got to their table like a pitbull was chasing his ass.

Did Nick say he liked this uninhibited side of Cassidy? He meant loved.

Chapter Seven

T*HIS IS REALLY happening.*

I'm going to have sex with Nick.

I'm going to see him naked.

He's going to see me naked.

Cassidy stiffened amid their tangle of arms and legs as they stumbled into their hotel room, mouths connected in a kiss that made her breathless.

Nick kicked the door shut with his foot, pulled back. "You okay?"

"Yes." She was. Mostly. It just now hit her that this wasn't only sex. Sharing her body with him meant sharing her deepest, darkest secret and shame. Sure, she could make this quick and dirty, leave her sweater on and keep her back against the wall or pressed into the couch, but she didn't do sex that way. It wasn't something meaningless to her, especially with Nick.

She stepped backward and before she chickened out, lifted the hem of her sweater up and over her head. Clutching the clothing in her hand, she kept taking steps back. He took steps forward. His gaze fell to her black lace bra before returning to her face. His incredible blue eyes told her this was going to be okay. She'd tell him what happened and then they'd carry on. The grim reminder of her past didn't get to be in charge anymore.

She'd never been this intimate this fast with someone before. With her two previous relationships she'd dated the guy for weeks first, told him about her past before they took things beyond PG rated make-outs. She hadn't wanted them caught unaware, more for her sake than theirs.

You've known Nick your whole life.

"You don't look so sure, Sid, and even though it would kill me to stop what we've started, nothing happens in this room that you don't want to have happen."

"This is going to happen." She affirmed. God, she wanted it to happen so badly. He brought out an uncontrolled, wanton side of her she liked. A lot.

"I can't give you more than right now, you understand that, right?"

"Yes." She tried to keep any emotion off her face, but must have failed because she saw concern etch a path around his eyes.

"This is all on me. I've still got shit to work out. I can't do long-term with anyone. But I want to breathe you in, every inch of you. I want to kiss you, taste you, and know what it feels like to be buried inside you. I can't remember ever wanting anyone so badly."

Her heart beat a rhythm like her favorite country song.

She couldn't either.

"And the way you look at me? Jesus, Sid. I'm going to earn that admiration by making you feel so damn good."

"S-sounds good to me. I just need to tell you something first."

"Okay," he said, flipping on the light switch and leaving space between them when the backs of her legs hit the bed in her room. She plopped down. "Should I take off my shirt first so we're on equal footing?"

How could she not adore this man for lightening the mood? "Yes. Yes you should."

He pulled it off one-handed, flung it to the side. She almost slid off the bed when she saw his bare torso. His broad shoulders alone were enough to make her woozy. Add in a muscled chest, toned abs, and the tops of those sexy V-cuts on his hipbone that made anatomy her new favorite subject, and she had to press her lips together to keep from moaning out loud.

It wasn't just his exceptional looks, though. She'd photographed gorgeous men without their shirts on, and not one had stirred anything inside her. With the man before her now, she wanted to lay her head on his chest, fall asleep to his heartbeats. His body offered pleasure *and* security in her foolishly smitten mind.

"Eyes up here while you talk, beautiful." He motioned to his chiseled face. Like *that* would help.

"My sophomore year of college I had my first boyfriend.

I met him at a fraternity party and for some reason he decided he liked me even though he could have his pick of girls since he was the quarterback of the football team." Nick's eyes widened at her disclosure, hinting that he thought a girl like her, from a small town with little in the way of worldliness, didn't fit with a Division I quarterback.

He'd be right.

"He had a reputation and was with a different girl every week," she said. "But once he laid eyes on me, he said I was it. I was flattered by the attention and fell hard and fast for him. He was sweet and funny and he loved that I had an interest in football and didn't get bored when he talked about it." She wrung her sweater in her hands.

Nick stayed perfectly still, his eyes locked on hers.

"Part of my appeal, I know, was I didn't put out right away, but after a month I gave him my virginity. The sex was great. I loved it and I loved him. One night he asked if he could blindfold me. I said yes. I was game for whatever he wanted to do. I trusted him. Another night he asked if he could tie my wrists. Again, I said okay.

"Then one night he was upset with me for getting drunk while out with my friends for my roommate's birthday. He and a few guys showed up at the bar we were at and he didn't like how friendly a group of frat boys were being so he asked me to leave with him. His frustration was obvious and I didn't want to make a scene so I did. When we got back to his place he took me straight to his bedroom. I was still feeling the effects of the alcohol and so I was pretty much putty in his hands."

Cass dropped her gaze to the carpeted floor. This was where the shame came in. The not knowing that Michael could be so cruel, that she'd put her trust in him and he'd destroyed it.

"We got undressed and he asked me to lay on the bed on my stomach. Then he tied my hands to the bed. When he straddled my hips instead of kissing my back like he usually did, I didn't think anything of it."

Nick shifted from one leg to the other, drawing her attention back to him. He took a step closer.

"He opened the drawer on the nightstand and I thought he was grabbing a condom, but he grabbed a box of matches instead."

Cass choked back the tears that still sometimes sprang when she remembered that night. Nick's sharp inhalation didn't help, but she managed to blink away the pain. She didn't want to cry over this again. She simply needed to share the circumstance of her scar with him so it didn't come up later. She'd gone through therapy. Called Rowan when she had the occasional breakdown. Had been with two men who treated her nicely.

She'd persevered. She was good.

"I didn't know my boyfriend had a thing for fire. And a thing for inflicting pain."

"Fuck." Nick dropped to his knees and clasped her hands

in his. In his eyes she saw a blaze of care—and rage.

"He told me I needed to be punished for the way I behaved. That *his* girlfriend didn't flirt with other guys. I hadn't flirted with anyone, but he wouldn't listen. He lit a match and put the flame on my lower back. I screamed for him to stop but he wouldn't. I tried to buck him off me, but I was still drunk and he weighed way more than I did."

Nick's hands squeezed hers. Tension rolled through the cords of his arm muscles like waves under his skin. His chest rose and fell and he let out a pained sigh.

"He let the match burn my skin until he had to blow it out or burn himself. Then he lit a second one. And a third. By that point I'd lost my fight and the pain was so unbearable I started to go into shock. The next thing I remember was waking up in the hospital."

"I'm so sorry."

"Michael told the doctor I'd gotten drunk, taken my clothes off to skinny dip and backed into a tiki torch at a party. The doctor believed him without question because when you're the quarterback of a national championship team everyone apparently thinks you're golden."

"Do not tell me that asshole didn't pay for what he did to you."

"He thought we'd just go back to being boyfriend and girlfriend. He told me he loved me, but that sometimes—"

"I don't want to hear it. I can't fucking hear it." Nick dropped his head.

Cassidy slipped her hand from his and lifted his chin. "I told him I didn't want him anywhere near me ever again and I was going to tell the truth. But he said if I told anyone it was him, he would make my life hell, starting with making sure I got the reputation as a slut who liked to be tied up and fucked in the ass."

"Goddammit," Nick said.

"I couldn't have handled that. I was nineteen and worried about what others thought. Trying to fit in. And I couldn't win against him, not with football on his side. So I let it go. Well, let him go. It took me two years of therapy to process everything and stop blaming myself. Sometimes I still do, though."

"I want to kill him."

"Thank you."

He cupped the back of her head with his left hand and brought her face to his chest. He held her there, like she'd imagined, and she closed her eyes. Several quiet minutes passed before she said, "I wanted to explain before you saw my scar."

His heart pounded underneath her cheek as he reached his right arm around her side. With a gentle touch, he caressed her lower back, his fingers finding and tracing the scar tissue. She shivered at the care he took. A piece of her heart latched on to him.

"Thanks for trusting me with this," he said quietly.

She lifted her head. For reasons she couldn't afford to

make sense of, she trusted Nick more than she trusted anyone else. "The idea of having sex with you has obviously muddled my brain."

His slow smile put flutters in her stomach. "Good thing no thinking will be required when you have sex with me."

"There's a joke in there somewhere but I'm slow on the uptake at the moment."

"You know what that calls for?"

She pursed her lips like a fish. "A one-on-one with Jimmy Fallon?"

"Damn, your mouth is sexy." He stood, gave his hand to help her up from the bed. "Dessert."

"And by dessert you mean you, right?"

He chuckled before palming her cheek and looking humorless said, "I'm glad you can joke so quickly after being so serious, but I need a little more time."

Oh.

"Oh."

Oh my. Nick truly cared about her.

Dropping his arm, he picked up her sweater from where it had fallen on the floor and handed it to her. "Get comfortable and I'll order something up."

Or maybe she repulsed him instead. He obviously wanted her body covered and for a few agonizing seconds she wondered if "time" meant he didn't want to see her scar. He'd lost people to fire. He'd no doubt seen burn victims. She sat back down on the edge of the bed to try and put on a calm facade. Perhaps he'd changed his mind and dessert was his way of putting space between them. She couldn't fault him for hating her wound if it brought him bad memories.

When he reached the doorway he looked over his shoulder, catching her in thought. "Hey," he said.

She gave him a weak smile and waved him on, worried that if she spoke her voice would crack and he'd know something bothered her. She was better off if nothing more happened between them. She didn't normally behave this way and how would she feel afterward? When Nick dropped her off at home tomorrow with a "see-ya" and nothing more.

Warm hands gripped her shoulders, igniting sparks of energy inside her. She hadn't realized he'd moved back into the room. Looking up, she found a man on a different mission from a minute ago. His expression held determination. Desire.

"I didn't back off because of your scar." He practically growled. "So kick that thought out of your head right now."

"O-okay."

He pushed her onto the mattress. She scooted back on her elbows as he put a knee on the bed and followed her, his rock-hard body looming over hers in the most sexy, heart-pounding way. "I wanted time to get *my* head on straight because I'm feeling protective and possessive and I want to fuck you until all you remember is me inside you, and you forget that piece of shit ever existed and ever touched you."

Cass trembled with arousal.

"And I'm worried that if we do this right now, I might be too rough for you because I'm feeling anything but gentle and it would fucking kill me to hurt you. You deserve to be cherished, Sid, your body worshipped with tenderness."

Her head reached the pillows. She stopped moving, relaxed her arms. He reached out to play with her hair, fanned out on the soft cotton. The unrushed gesture had her body completely yielding to him.

"We have all night for that," she said in a sultry whisper she didn't recognize. The red-hot desire thrumming through her wasn't like anything she'd experienced before.

"I'm excellent at all night." At his cocky grin she stifled a nervous giggle.

"So take me right now, Nick. I won't break. I promise." She raked her fingers over his shoulders and down the backs of his arms. "I need you inside me."

"Done." He unbuttoned her pants, slid them off her legs, taking her shoes, too, and left her in nothing but her lace bra and panties. His gaze raked over her, the appreciation in his deep blue eyes raising goose bumps on her skin.

He kissed the center of her stomach, her cleavage, her neck. "I'm going to take good care of you," he said in her ear before he rolled her onto her stomach.

She hitched in a breath at the new position, conscious of the discolored, irregular fibrous skin at the base of her spine. Nick pressed his lips to her nape while he raised her arms above her head. "Your body is made to endure, Sid, but more than that, its purpose is to soar and, when I look at you, I see someone with strong, beautiful wings."

Oh, my God. She silently repeated his words and tucked them into her heart and mind so she'd always have them—for later. Because right now all she could concentrate on was the drag of his tongue and press of his lips down the sensitive flesh of her spine. He got to her bra strap, and with one flick of his fingers had it unclasped. His hands splayed over her waist as he continued to lick and kiss his way lower.

Tingles of pleasure followed his mouth. Her vision flew out of focus. Liquid heat pooled between her thighs.

When he reached her scar, he didn't stop or falter. He kissed it from corner to corner, seemingly unaffected by the raised, ugly skin. She turned her head to look down at him. He glanced up at her. In the sparkling blue depths staring back at her, she saw lust and affection, and every doubt she had disappeared.

Now that they'd taken care of that, a switch seemingly turned on in Nick because his hands and mouth traveled over her backside with urgency. He hooked his fingers in the sides of her panties and tugged them down and off. Then he kissed his way up her legs, ran his tongue over the insides of her thighs. She involuntarily lifted her hips, seeking his attention in her most intimate spot. He cupped her there, ran his thumb over her swollen flesh, and lavished her back with open-mouthed affection.

She buried her face in the pillow to keep from moaning

like a wanton woman who hadn't had sex in way too long.

Which she was.

"Don't," he said. "Don't stifle your sounds. I want to hear all of your noises while I make you come." Then he slid a finger inside her, pulling a loud breathless sigh from her parted lips.

He groaned and expertly worked her inside and out with his talented fingers. At the sounds of her wetness, her arousal intensified. She spread her legs wider. She'd never been more turned on.

Until he slipped down the bed, wrapped his arms around her thighs, and closed his mouth over her. She bucked, her hips lifting to give him better access. He licked from her slit to her engorged clitoris. The sensation was so potent she couldn't have stopped her moans of pleasure if she'd tried. She'd never been tasted like this before. The position, combined with the wet heat of Nick's lips and tongue, were too much. He sucked, made his own sexy sound of enjoyment, and that was all it took for her to shatter into the longest orgasm of her life.

"Now I want to feel you do that around my cock." Nick rasped, flipping her over onto her back. He shucked his jeans and boxer briefs and pulled a condom out of the wallet in his discarded pants.

Cass wiggled out of her bra, her gaze stuck on Nick's magnificent erection. And by magnificent, she meant magnum. Her insides went tight and hot in anticipation of feeling him fill her.

"Don't worry. It'll fit," he said with a gleam in his eyes.

"I'm not worried," she said, sitting up and gripping his smooth, hard length in her hand. "I'm excited."

Nick jolted at her touch, his stomach muscles shifted. "Lay back, Sid."

His rough, commanding tone reminded her of the shiver down her back when she'd heard his sexy voice behind her at the riverbank. Something in the way he spoke sent a ribbon of heat straight to her core. She didn't hesitate to follow his order. Didn't hesitate to run her hands over her breasts, down her stomach and across her thighs, slowly parting her legs in invitation.

"Don't keep me waiting," she said.

"Trust me," he said, sheathing himself before crawling onto the bed so he once again had her underneath him. "I won't. I just need a quick taste of this." He dipped his head to take her nipple into his mouth.

Desire slammed into her. She arched her back, seeking more. Nick delivered with lashes from his tongue at the same time he hooked her right leg over his shoulder. She threaded her fingers through his dark hair, groaned in pleasure.

She felt sexy, desired, cherished in a way she'd only dreamed of. *Enjoy the dream, because it isn't going to last.*

He lifted his head as if he'd heard her thought. She got lost in the twin pools of vibrant, energetic blue, and, for several charged seconds, they stared at each other. Their involvement had an expiration date, but in his eyes she saw she wasn't the only one affected by this unexpected draw between them.

"You're unbelievably sexy, Sid," he said before he closed his mouth over her other breast.

As he sucked and pulled the taut peak between his teeth, the tip of his cock nudged her opening. Then, raining kisses between her breasts and up the column of her neck, he slid inside her. She lifted her hips to meet his slow thrust, wanting him deeper faster.

He obliged, stretching and filling her so fully, tingly sensations covered every inch of her inside and out. Nick moved with swift, powerful strokes, touching a place she'd never been touched before. Literally. She smiled at the turn of her thoughts over his size.

"You feel so good," she said.

"I was thinking the same thing about you."

"Yeah?"

Rather than answer, he took her bottom lip between his teeth. Kissed her jawline, the shell of her ear. He adjusted his angle slightly, lifted her leg higher over his shoulder.

"Oh, God," she said through a heavy breath. She dug her nails into his back as *his* labored breathing and firm, steely rhythm added to her eagerness.

He continued to drive into her, each exquisite thrust more potent than the last. Then he pressed up onto his hands, knocking her leg off his shoulder, and rolled his hips in delicious circles against her. She looked down at where their bodies joined. Nick noticed, and with a sexy grin, slowed his tempo. He pulled out almost all the way before plunging back in. Did it again. Watching him pump inside her intensified her connection to him. He filled her with one swift motion, pulled back, did it again. She thought she'd die from the perfect pleasure of it.

She clung to his back and chased her second orgasm, yet, at the same, time she wanted to make this last as long as possible. Nothing compared to the incredible feeling of having Nick buried deep inside her. But when his movements grew more insistent and he sank into her, she tumbled toward the finish line. She rocked against him as she cried out, her climax so consuming it raced through her entire body.

Nick groaned and followed right behind, shuddering with his own release.

Afterward, he collapsed onto his back beside her. They lay quietly, exhaling in satisfaction. Nick took her hand in his and held it in the space between them on the comforter, which did all sorts of fluttery things to her insides.

"So," she said softly, peeking at him out of the corner of her eye, "is it too soon to ask that we do that again?"

He smiled and turned his head to look at her. "Not too soon at all." He rolled to his side, pushed up onto his elbow. "In fact, I think this might be a good time for me to collect on my animal cracker win."

Cassidy scrunched up her nose. He gave a short laugh that took away all her annoyance at losing the bet. The sexy sound, combined with his adorable simper, was enough to erase everything that had ever bothered her about him. "Oh?"

"I say we do this again *and again*. I can pull an all-nighter. You?"

She tried to look put off even though she was anything but. She was the queen of all-nighters, often working without sleep after a day of picture taking that really excited her. Nick was a subject that most definitely gave her a buzz.

"If I must," she said on a dramatic sigh.

He also posed a serious threat to her heart, but she'd worry about that tomorrow after they'd gone their separate ways.

Chapter Eight

NICK STOOD UNDER the warm water spewing out of the showerhead. Leaning with his hands on the tiled wall, he watched the soap bubbles disappear down the drain. Tired, his muscles ached in a good way. Not the same way they'd felt used last weekend, but better than he'd wanted them to. He and Code had spent the morning and better part of the afternoon mountain biking on a stretch of cliff trails about as wide as a two-by-four with a steep drop off that would give most people nightmares.

The last thing Nick had wanted to do was something risky. He'd planned to live a safer, quieter existence, but people kept pulling him back to the ledge. And damn it, he'd discovered he still thrived on the exposure to danger. Risk was in his blood whether he liked it or not. Today with Code, the getaway with Sid, they both reminded him adventure made life more interesting.

Sid.

He hadn't seen or talked to her since dropping her off at home last Sunday, but she'd be here tonight for his dad's sixtieth birthday party. A little voice in the back of his head told him to keep his distance. The devil on his shoulder told him to get close. After the sub fire, he'd decided he only wanted to exist for himself from here on out, but Sid had him rethinking that vow.

Talk about dangerous.

Not that he wanted to extend his relationship with her. He didn't. Maybe he *could* go back to firefighting, though. Go back to being part of a team on the front lines. His best efforts may have fallen short on the sub, but that didn't mean they would the next time.

The water turned lukewarm, signaling he'd been standing under the shower spray for a long damn time. His parents had remodeled the bathroom a few years ago, installing a larger water heater and replacing the pipes so that they no longer made noise loud enough to give away his location. He'd needed to disappear for a bit while Rowan and his mom flew around downstairs like tiny tornados in preparation for the party tonight.

He shut off the water and stepped out of the shower to dry off before tying the towel around his waist. A quick brush of his teeth followed. He turned to open the bathroom door, but someone beat him to it.

The door flew open, keeping him rooted to his spot. He rested against the counter in fascination as Sid spun into the small room and rushed to close the door behind her. She locked it, then leaned her forehead and palms on the wood panel. Her shoulders sagged as if in relief. She wore her light brown hair pulled back into a pretty ponytail. The pale green strapless dress cinched at her waist and flared out at her hips like an umbrella that stopped mid-thigh. His gaze slid down toned, smooth legs. He remembered licking his way up them to get to her wet center. He'd never been with a woman who responded like she did to his touch. Hell, his voice alone seemed to get her hot and bothered.

Images of her naked and under him, riding him, bent over the couch, in the shower, filled his head in perfect clarity. The scent of her skin, the perspiration that made their bodies slick as they moved together. He glanced down. Shit. She had him hard and they hadn't even made eye contact yet.

He cleared his throat.

She yelped and bumped her head on the door in surprise before whirling around to face him. One hand flew to her chest, the other to rub her hairline. "Ow. Holy crap, you scared me! What are you doing in here?"

He raised his eyebrows. She didn't really need him to answer that, did she?

Her gaze fell to his bare chest, then lower, where she definitely got a view of what she did to him.

"Oh, my God. I'm so sorry I interrupted you, uh, about to masturbate. I didn't hear anyone in here so didn't think to knock. I'll just go back out the way I came." She gestured with her thumb over her smooth, naked shoulder. "Forget you even saw me and I'll forget I saw you. This doesn't have to be weird or anything. It's not like I haven't seen you—never mind, I'll just go now and see you downstairs when you're, uh, through doing you know…that." Her eyes dipped to his towel one more time.

"Hang on," he said, half-intrigued by her adorable nervousness and half put off that she didn't think she had anything to do with his predicament. Granted, what reason would she have to think she affected him this way given he'd made zero contact with her this past week.

Which, again, made him a total dick. They were friends and he'd treated her the way he swore not, like a hookup.

"I'm not rubbing one off." He took two steps, putting him close enough to carefully rub his fingers across the top of her forehead. "You okay?"

Her breath hitched. "I'm fine."

"You sure?"

She nodded and bit the corner of her mouth—a mouth he knew could get him off in minutes. The memory of her sucking him deep, her warm lips wrapped his throbbing cock, flashed in his mind. Jesus. How was he going to make it through the night in front of his family without giving away he and Sid had done dirty things to each other?

"So this is a normal state for you then?" She teased, self-assured Sid back in front of him.

"It's a problem I seem to have whenever you're around."

"Really?" she said surprised, but with a glint in her eye.

"Proof's right down there, beautiful." He took a step

back before he tried to do something stupid with that proof. They were in his parents' house. And there weren't supposed to be any repeat performances from their weekend away.

"Kind of *hard* to miss," she managed around a giggle.

He grinned. A guy didn't mind jokes about his size.

"So, what are you doing in here?" He tightened the towel around his waist.

"Oh, I came in here to hide for a few."

That didn't compute at all in Nick's head. Who did she need to hide from?

"From your sister. I haven't seen or talked to her all week and she wanted to know about our trip to Jackson Hole. I told her about skydiving and the wildlife tour easy enough, but you know Ro. She went into reporter mode and started asking for every little detail and I started to sweat. I got worried she'd be able to tell we had sex so I rushed out of the kitchen saying I'd eaten something bad for lunch."

"Would it be a bad thing if she found out?" In his mind it certainly was, but he found himself curious about how Sid felt on the topic.

She titled her head, gave him a look that said *really*? "She thought we were the perfect auction date because we could keep our hands to ourselves. She's worried you're still healing from the sub fire. She thought she could trust me to take care with you."

"And you?"

"And me what?"

"Did she think I'd be careful with you?"

"Yes."

But he hadn't been. Not entirely. He'd taken his sister's best friend to bed and been anything but cautious in multiple sexual positions. Knowing she felt things for him he didn't feel in return. Yes, they were two consenting adults and Sid was an intelligent woman who knew what she was doing—was eager to do it even. But that didn't make it right.

He jammed his fingers through his wet hair. Despite what was right, he wanted more. He felt drawn to her in a way he couldn't explain. In close confines like they were in now, the pull intensified. Her gorgeous face and body made him crave to be skin to skin. But her intelligent, green eyes and what lay behind them stirred a kind of insatiable desire that made him weak in the knees.

"I'll leave you to your hiding then."

"Okay."

Instead of winding around each other, they ended up bumping into one another. "Sorry," they muttered in unison and tried again, only to take matching steps a second time. Sid put her palm on his chest to catch her balance.

His skin caught fire at her touch. He put his hands on her hips and spun her around, trapping her between the sink and himself.

"Thanks," she said, darting a quick glance at his mouth.

"No problem."

With their bodies lined up, neither made motion to move. Technically, Nick should back away, but he couldn't seem to get the memo to his feet.

"I heard you did a check on all the fire detectors at the high school," she said, indicating she didn't want this conversation to end either.

"Yeah. Mitch asked me to help out." Mitch Holden had taken over coaching duties from Coach D a few years ago. Every year, Mitch had the football players contribute something to the school and this year had been a safety inspection of the fire alarms. Nick had been happy to lead the team over two afternoons and talk about his experience as a navy firefighter since a few of the boys had expressed interest in joining the military and/or firefighting.

"That was nice of you." She put her hands on the counter, hoisted herself into a sitting position atop the cream-colored marble.

He took the opportunity to check out her dress, the dusts of sparkle across her collarbone from her lotion, Nick guessed, and the way the bodice pushed her full breasts up. "You look really pretty today."

"Thank you. Green is my favorite color."

As of right now it was his, too. His fingers itched to wander underneath her skirt to find out if she wore matching underwear. *Bad idea, bud.* He took a small step back, tightened the towel again.

Her gaze tracked down his body. He felt it like a stroke.

God damn, what this girl did to him. "You should probably go get dressed."

"Probably."

"But?" She'd heard the 'but' in his tone.

One corner of his mouth quirked up. "I'm wondering if there are any condoms in here."

"Nick!" She chided, but her eyes whispered *yes please*. Sid continued to surprise and delight him in ways he'd never imagined.

"I don't think there are," he said. "Which is for the best."

"Right." Disappointment flooded the one word. "We decided what happened in Jackson Hole stays in Jackson Hole."

He put his hands on her dress-covered thighs, but one little flick of the material and he'd be able to touch skin. "True, but that's not why."

"It isn't?"

"No. It's best if we do this again somewhere without the risk of interruption."

A thick swallow made its way down her throat. "So you want to have sex again?"

The last thing in the world he wanted was to hurt her, so he'd let her choose. "I want to make you feel good. I want you to make me feel good. How we do that is up to you."

"You busy later? After the party?"

"I don't think so."

"Good. My smoke detector needs a new battery and I

can't reach it. Think you could come give me a hand?"

He knew she meant that as play on words, but all he could think of as he stumbled back was Sloane. Dying in a house fire because they didn't have adequate detectors.

All of a sudden heat licked the back of his neck. He couldn't breathe.

"Nick?" Sid reached her hand out.

"I've got to go," he said gruffly and bolted out of the room. When he got to the guest bedroom he paced back and forth.

Yeah, he'd thought of Sloane, but the image of her had lasted all of two seconds if he were honest with himself. What bothered him more was the picture of Sid that chased Sloane away. Cassidy was inside his head and the thought of something bad happening to her sucked the air out of his lungs.

Not the position he wanted to be in.

Not ever again.

"WHAT'S GOING ON with you and my brother?"

Cassidy jumped at the sound of Rowan's voice over her shoulder. Raspberry lemonade went down the wrong pipe and the glass in Cass's hand clinked against her front teeth. She choked down the sweet drink, sputtering in the process, then used her free hand to wipe her mouth before turning to her best friend. "How is it you are the loudest person I know, yet you can sneak up on me without making a sound?"

"It's called talent." Ro patted Sid's back in comfort. Or maybe it was shrewdness because she added, "I can also tell when people are avoiding me."

"I'm not avoiding you," Cass lied.

"Nick's avoiding me, too, which leads me to believe there is more to your weekend getaway than you're letting on."

Cass tried to look innocent by shrugging and making an I've-no-idea-what-you're-talking-about face. Rowan responded with an I'm-on-to-you expression, her blue eyes narrowed just enough to mean business.

Which made Cass feel both nervous and guilty. She'd cave eventually, tell Ro everything, but not during the birthday party. She and Ro stood outside on the patio with happy chaos going on around them. Family and friends were eating, drinking, and playing backyard games set up to make Dennis Palotay feel like a kid again. "You should move with me to LA or New York. Your nose for news is wasted on a small town newspaper."

"Right?" Rowan said, a big smile on her face.

"We could be roommates."

Rowan's delicate features softened. "Wait. You're serious? You want me to go with you?"

"I'd love for you to." Cass hadn't thought about it until now, but why not? Opportunities abounded for both of them in a bigger city. And having each other to prop up and lean on while they furthered their dreams took all the worry out of navigating a new home base.

"We would have so much fun."

"There's an offer on my parents' house. I—we—could be on our way in forty-five days. Or less, really, once I move everything out. I'm free to go whenever, but remember I travel a lot so you'll be alone sometimes."

Rowan planted her hands on her chest, one palm on top of the other. "My heart is pounding," she said. "I love this idea."

"The *Times* would be lucky to have you."

"Which one?"

"I'm leaning toward LA. What say you, my partner in fun?"

"I say you are the best and smartest friend ever. I'll start sending resumes next week." She bounced up and down with excitement, but stopped abruptly when her dad gave her a thumbs up from across the patio. Looked like he'd just scored the winning beanbag toss. "Let's not say anything to anyone yet."

"My lips are sealed."

"Yeah. About that, Miss Redirect. Back to my original question, what's up with you and Nick? He keeps staring at you."

"What? No he doesn't." Sid glanced around the yard until she found Nick talking to Paige Griffin. Their eyes met briefly before he turned his attention back to Paige. She kept touching his arm while she talked non-stop. "Looks to me like he's having a great time with Paige."

Rowan shot her a suspicious look. "Is that jealously I hear in your voice?"

"Not in the least. Just stating a fact." At least she didn't think it was jealousy that had her grinding her teeth together.

Nick could talk to whomever he wanted. But Paige was selfish and so wrapped up in her own world, she didn't even have the common courtesy to help someone pick up their dropped groceries. Paige stepped over oranges rolling down the parking lot and tampons strewn all over the ground. Cass had firsthand knowledge of this.

So it bothered her a little that she seemed to be charming Nick.

"Well you're wrong. He's miserable at the moment," Ro said.

"I'm pretty sure the smile on his face proves contrary."

"Nope. That's a counterfeit smile. I studied his expressions and mannerisms for years before he left home so I'd know how to read when a guy was bullshitting me and right now my dear brother is smiling because he's polite, but inside he wishes a hole would open up in the grass and suck Paige into it."

Cassidy studied Nick. His brows did seem to be pinched ever so slightly. "How many smiles does he have? And how come you never told me this?"

"He's got a few, and I thought I had told you. Oh wait,

it was Hayley that I told one night senior year when she was upset about something Cody had said or did, and we talked shit about guys and drank tequila to make her feel better.

"What are some of the smiles?" Cass thought back to the ones Nick had given her. They all seemed to say the same thing. What that was, she didn't know, probably because his straight white teeth and creases around his mouth made her light-headed. She couldn't think about anything other than his handsome face when he smiled.

Rowan lifted her hand and ticked off the names with her fingers. "I know it all, I'm the Boss, Up-to-No-Good, Counterfeit, Dealer."

"Dealer?"

"He gives that one when he doesn't feel like being polite and wants to deal with you later."

Paige laughed at something Nick said, her fingertips brushing his arm like she was enthralled and he was the funniest guy she'd ever met.

"Come on. Let's go save him." Rowan grabbed Cassidy's hand, leaving her no choice but to tag along on this rescue mission. "Hey, guys. Paige, your mom needs you to be her badminton partner."

Cassidy glanced in the direction of the badminton net. Sure enough, Paige's mom stood without a partner.

"Why me?" Paige asked, clearly wanting to stay next to Nick.

Rowan shrugged one shoulder before she looked away

and waved her arm to get Mrs. Griffin's attention. Once she had it, Ro made a gesture toward Paige and Mrs. Griffin enthusiastically nodded her head. "All I know is, she'll be very disappointed if you don't head over there quickly."

"Fine." Paige relented, then much sweeter said, "I'll see you Thursday, Nick." She touched his arm *again* and sauntered off.

What were she and Nick doing on Thursday? Did they have a date? Cass hated that she cared what Nick did with his free time. And whom he did it with.

"Hey, you three," Dennis said, saving Cass from any more troublesome thoughts. "You're up."

Rowan gave her dad a sideways hug. "What are we up for?"

"Passing practice. Come on."

Nick fell in step beside her as they followed Dennis and Ro toward a giant blue tarp that hung between two trees. Nick's arm brushed hers as they walked. She liked the simple touch way more than she should have.

There were several different sized squares cut into the tarp, each one lined with colorful duct tape and assigned a different point value. Nick picked up the football sitting on the grass.

"Five throws. The person with the most points wins," Ro said with a competitive edge to her voice.

"You're on." Nick palmed the ball like it would do anything he wanted it to, even with his eyes closed. Which was the only way anyone had a chance against him.

"How about we make that teams?" Dennis said, picking up on his children's rivalry.

Ro never stopped believing she could best her older brother. And occasionally she did. But Cass was pretty sure Nick gave those wins away because he loved his sister something fierce. Rowan often thought Nick an overprotective skunk, but what Cassidy wouldn't give to have someone always looking out for her.

"Ro Lo and I against you two."

"Dad obviously knows which Palotay has mad skills," Rowan teased, snagging the football out of Nick's hands. "Birthday boy's team goes first."

"Sid and I could beat you two blindfolded," Nick said.

And Cassidy's mind immediately went to the bedroom and Nick blindfolding her before he had his wicked way with her.

"And give you an excuse when you lose? I don't think so," Ro said. She handed the football to her dad. "You're up young man."

Nick leaned over, his mouth dangerously close to Cassidy's ear. "You know how to throw a football, right?"

Um, wrong. Cass didn't have a superstar football older brother who taught her how to throw one. "Of course."

Dennis scored ten points on his first throw. Nick scored twenty, the ball sailing through the smallest cut out, and thus worth the most points. Rowan added ten on her turn.

Cassidy held the football in her hands. Yes, *hands*. She couldn't decide which one to use. Sometimes her ambidexterity didn't send a clear signal to her brain and it took her a little extra time to commit. She threw a basketball with her left hand, a baseball with her right. Cut her food with her right. Wrote with her left.

"You going to let go of that sometime soon?" Nick asked.

"Right now." She aimed for the largest circle and launched the ball with her right hand. It missed the target and landed—

"Ow!" someone said from behind the tree.

It landed on a party guest. Great. She'd missed the tarp entirely. "Sorry!" Cassidy shouted, running around the tree to retrieve the ball and make sure the person was okay. She hurried back and handed the ball off to Dennis.

Dennis gave her a "good try." Rowan attempted to stop laughing. And Nick? He looked both anguished *and* entertained.

"Oops," Cass said apologetically.

When it came to her turn again, Nick showed her the proper way to hold a football. He placed her fingers in the right positions along the white lace and wrapped her thumb around the ball. His gentle, but firm touch combined with an attentive tone of voice raised the pedestal she had him on even higher.

She imagined him teaching her all sorts of things.

Her second throw failed to fly through its mark, but at

least the football hit the tarp. Nick winked at her. She nodded, then quickly looked away before she did something stupid like make lovesick eyes at him.

Five minutes later, they'd lost the game and Rowan's bragging rights pushed Nick to seek out other company. Cassidy didn't interact with him for the rest of the night.

Reminding her that some things were best left alone.

Chapter Nine

LATE THURSDAY AFTERNOON, Cassidy squeezed her hands around the steering wheel of the borrowed pickup truck and prayed she made it to the gas station next to the Get 'n Go. Running out of gas on the side of Highway 89 was not on her list of things to do today.

"Come on, baby, just a couple more miles."

She'd spent the warm, sunny day honoring her parents' request that the furniture in the house be donated to those in need. In her bittersweet travels and stops to take pictures, she'd neglected to keep an eye on the fuel gauge. She had one more delivery outside of town and no idea how long she'd been driving on fumes, the distance to empty reading zero on the console.

"No, no, no." She chanted when she pressed on the accelerator and to her dismay, the truck slowed. A freaking block from the gas station, the truck stalled.

The good news? She was only a block away and could walk to get one of those red plastic gas cans to help her out.

The bad news? She looked around the front seat and discovered she'd left her purse...somewhere. She closed her eyes and remembered seeing it sitting on the kitchen counter. It wasn't the first time she'd forgotten to take it with her.

She ran across the highway to take her chances on borrowing some gasoline with a promise to return, rather than call a friend for help.

"Need a lift?" Nick said from over her shoulder, startling her.

His deep voice had been etched into her permanent memory bank after he'd helped her up at the riverbank. Dropping her hand from the station's glass door, she spun around. "What makes you think I need a lift?"

"The truck across the way." He lifted his chin in the direction of the white pick up.

That he'd noticed her sent a shiver down her back. "It's just a gas problem."

"It's too bad there aren't warning lights to prevent that," he said good-naturedly.

She stepped away from the door as a customer exited the small building. "Like you always obey warnings."

"True. But I'm very good at following orders. Especially when they benefit someone else." The playful quirk of his sexy mouth combined with those bedroom eyes of his sent her mind straight to the gutter. Which no doubt had been his intention.

Her nipples hardened. *Don't stop, Nick. Oh, God, yes! Right there. I'm going to come.* He'd most definitely listened to her directions in bed. "I'd like to argue that point with you, but I can't."

He reached out to comb his fingers through her hair. She went completely still. "Looks like you've been out in nature again," he said, pulling a leaf from her strands and steering the conversation to a safer topic.

"A tree house actually."

At his arched brow she added, "I've spent the day making furniture deliveries and at one of my stops I met a little boy who wanted to show me his tree house." She rambled on about the sweet kid and staying to eat cookies and milk with him. Continued with the closing date of escrow on her parents' house and how nice it was to see their belongings make someone else's day. She wanted to keep talking to Nick even though her heart told her she should walk away.

"Come on, then," he said when she paused to take a breath.

"Come on where?"

"Let's get you gas and I'll help with your last delivery." He left no room for argument, insisting he could leave his car at the Get 'n Go.

The nice young man behind the gas station counter recognized Nick and said it was an honor to meet a real life hero. He gave Nick the plastic gas can and said there would be no charge for the gallon of gas. A military courtesy, the guy added, his eyes wide with admiration. Nick said thanks and smiled appreciatively, but Cass sensed his unease with the high regard all the way back to the truck.

The tension broke when she drove into the gas station and asked Nick if he wouldn't mind springing for a full tank because she'd forgotten her wallet. He'd found that highly amusing. "Does that happen often?" he asked.

"Only here in Marietta."

"It's a good thing we ran into each other, then."

Their good timing continued when they got to their destination. The older couple's grandson had had to go, leaving Cass grateful she had Nick to help unload the chair and ottoman. Climbing back into the truck after saying goodbye to the kind couple, she dropped her head and thought back on the day with a mix of gratification and melancholy.

Nick tucked a finger under her chin to lift her face toward his. "You did a good thing today. It's not easy to say goodbye to your childhood home."

It wasn't. Not at all. Despite her sheltered upbringing, tons of wonderful memories had been made inside those four walls.

"I like to do nice things for people."

"I know you do. It's an insanely attractive quality of yours." His eyes held hers, raising the temperature in the cab a thousand degrees.

She turned the key in the ignition. "Thank you. I could say the same to you."

"Have you decided which coast you're headed to?" And just like that the temperature dropped. Not because she wasn't excited about moving, but because it reminded her she and Nick were headed in different directions.

"Los Angeles."

"I can picture you there."

"Me, too." The other night she and Rowan had found a couple of places available for rent and had the best time laughing and making plans.

"Mind if I take a quick detour?" she asked after a few minutes of quiet.

He glanced at his watch. She'd never thought timepieces sexy before, but seeing the thick, black band around his tanned wrist made her squirm in her seat. "Go for it."

"I'm not keeping you from anything important, am I?"

"Nope."

"I've got an assignment that isn't due for a couple of weeks, but the lighting is perfect right now and I think the schedule I got said there's a class at this time." She turned off the highway onto a dirt lane marked by a small wooden sign with the name Pinecrest Road.

"Class?"

"Yoga." Sure enough, up ahead she saw a group of exercisers in a small clearing. She parked a short distance away to keep her arrival secret. The best images were captured when her subjects didn't know they were being photographed. "You can wait here if you want. I won't be too long." She grabbed her camera from the back seat of the double cab before hopping out into the pine-scented air.

Nick stepped on a twig beside her.

"Shh," she whispered, glad for his company. "I'd like to keep our presence unknown."

He nodded, his steps the rest of the way lighter than hers. Must have been his military training.

The class of six followed the instructor's silent movements, holding each pose in unspoken synchronicity. Emerald and lime green trees bookmarked the glade. A slow moving stream with jagged gray rocks granted both peace and awareness behind the teacher.

Cassidy clicked away. She lost track of time. Lost track of Nick. Only when the class ended did she lift her head from her work. Nick stood a few feet away with his hands in the front pockets of his jeans. She had no idea what his expression said.

"What?" she asked.

"You're fun to watch."

Seriously? He had to be messing with her. "While I work?"

"Then, too."

Her cheeks heated against her will, the memory of their night together slamming into her. "Come on, creeper," she said to cut the sexual tension. "It's time to go."

He tipped his head so his mouth almost touched her ear as they walked side by side. "You like to be watched. It turns you on."

She lifted her shoulder to rub his warm breath off her ear. "I don't think so."

"I know so. I also know watching you turns me on."

Oh, Lord. She had no defenses against this man. Pressure built between her thighs, a full-body flush made her skin tingle. "Did you know outdoor yoga adds a different dimension to the practice and strengthens a person's link with nature? By putting your body into the shape of a tree, or stretching your arms to mimic the graceful wingspan of bird, or breathing with the same cyclical sense as a body of water, you can evoke a feeling of harmony and connection to the universe." She put her camera in the backseat of the cab, closed the rear door, and turned around.

Nick stood *right there*. He trapped her against the truck, his arms extended on either side of her body to keep her in place. "I know what I want to be connected to."

Cassidy chewed her bottom lip.

"I can't stop thinking about you, Sid."

I can't stop thinking about you either. "Yeah?" She took the initiative and slipped her hands underneath his shirt. His stomach muscles flexed against the pads of her fingers as she did a little exploring.

"This is Colt Ewing's old pick up, right?" he asked.

"Yes."

"Let's see if our secret stash is still there." Nick put his hands on her hips and lifted her off the ground to spin her away from the truck.

"What are you talking about?"

Nick looked over his shoulder at her while he folded the

back seat. "Back in high school, we kept condoms in this storage compartment." He lifted the lid and looked inside. "Score."

"Is this your way of saying you want in my pants right here?" She glanced around. The yoga class had cleared out, twilight lengthened shadows.

He pulled the box out of the floor bin. "After that speech you gave about yoga and nature, I realized if I want to hit my idyllic spot, then I need to be inside you." He curled his finger around the belt loop of her jeans to tug her closer. "Deep inside you."

If a shiver could shiver, that was what happened to her at hearing his words and landing flush against his warm, hard body. "There's just one little problem," she murmured.

"Lay it on me."

"Aren't those over a decade old?" She squinted at the condom box.

"Shit. Let's check the expiration date." He let go of her pants and read the side of the box.

Cassidy laughed. "There is no way they are still good."

"You're right." The defeatist tone of his voice was too cute. He tossed the condoms into the truck bed.

"Lucky for you, I may have a solution." She wanted Nick inside her again so badly she ached with it. She'd known him her whole life. Trusted him not to hurt her. Physically, at least. Her heart argued this temporary understanding would leave permanent marks. Still, she pressed her hips against his, draped her arms around his neck. Skimming her lips along his jawline, his shudder made her surer of her offer. "I'm on the pill and clean. Tell me you're healthy, too, and then take me against this truck."

Having him inside her without any barrier was probably a stupid thing to do, but right now stupid sounded a lot better than being smart.

His hands palmed her ass. He pulled her tighter, the bulge in his jeans firmly in place at her sweet spot. "Had a check-up last month. I'm safe." He groaned.

Eyes locked on one another, Cass saw hot need and attraction and knew her gaze mirrored his. He sure as heck wasn't safe, not when he owned a growing piece of her heart, but hidden away on this beautiful piece of land under the canopy of aged trees, they could forget the outside world existed. Lose themselves to each other again.

"You sure?" he asked.

"Positive."

He lifted her off the ground. "Wrap your legs around me." She did and a second later he had her bottom on the edge of the backseat. "I'm afraid this is going to be quick." He kissed down the column of her neck, her head falling back in pleasure.

"Thank, God."

His lips curled into a smile against her skin. He worked the button and zipper on her pants while his mouth stayed busy on her collarbone. Cassidy pressed her hands into the seat cushion behind her, arched her back. The open collar of her white top left plenty more skin for him to explore.

"Lift up for me," he said.

She raised her butt. He slid her jeans down her hips and legs. When he reached her boots, he tugged them off. They hit the ground with a thump. Her pants followed with a tiny rustle as they landed on top of her shoes.

Nick undid his jeans and freed his erection, stroking it as he did so. It made her wet to watch him. Made her breathless with anticipation, her core muscles clench with need. He stepped between her legs, wrapped his hand around her right thigh to lift it, and proceeded to kiss the bejesus out of her mouth. Lips, tongue, teeth, he kissed her like he'd never get enough. She loved it.

His cock rubbed over her panties, setting off shocks of enjoyment. Unable to help herself, she ground against him, lost in sensations only he gave her. With his free hand, he traced his fingers down her side, leaving quivers underneath her shirt. She moaned inside his mouth.

He made a guttural sound from the back of his throat in response, and slipped his hand between his cock and her wet panties. He caressed her over the thin material, making her crazy, making her so aroused she bit his bottom lip.

He lifted his head. "You are so fucking hot."

Then he moved her underwear to the side and with one powerful thrust, buried himself inside her. She screamed out in pleasure. The feel of him without any latex was incredible.

It took him all of a minute to bring her close to orgasm. Each hungry surge of his hips lit her up inside with burning hot pulses. When she came with a dizzying explosion of feeling, he stilled, held her in his arm, and whispered, "I want to feel you do that again."

His movements after that varied between fast and faster. He lifted her knee higher, buried his face in her neck where he worshipped her with openmouthed kisses.

She moaned, sighed, panted, as he worked her toward another climax.

"I love the sounds you make," he said, voice husky.

"I love that you make me make them." She managed, just before she shouted his name and tumbled over into a second mind-blowing release.

Nick lasted another few seconds before his frenzied, powerful rocking stopped and she felt him throb inside her as he let go. She dug her fingers into his lower back to keep him right where he was. Not that he made any motion to pull out, but she didn't want this connection to end.

Cassidy looked over his head to their surroundings. With the truck door open wide, Nick's pants hanging off his very fine rear end, and her tucked just inside the cab with a bare leg wrapped around his waist, she imagined they painted a very interesting picture should someone come along.

A giggle slipped between her pressed lips.

"Not the reaction a guy wants to hear after delivering two orgasms." Nick lifted himself away.

Cool air wrapped around her at the loss of body heat. She slid her panties back into place, feeling the sticky reminder of what they'd just done, and not sorry in the least. She'd clean up at home.

"I was just imagining the picture we'd make if someone caught us right now," she said.

He zipped up, bent to grab her jeans. "A damn good one. Give me your foot."

She extended her leg. He pulled her pants over one foot, then the other, easing them up until they reached her thighs. She hopped out of the truck to wiggle them the rest of the way up. Nick knelt to help her with her boots.

"Do you always think in pictures?" he asked.

"Not all the time, but it's such a huge part of who I am sometimes I can't help it." He stared at her like she'd offered the answer to a question festering inside him for a long time. She put her hand on his chest. "You're wrong, though. It would have been a damn *fantastic* one."

"Which begs repeating." He took her wrist, kissed her knuckles. "Only at your place."

"Inviting yourself over?"

Apology, greed, longing, all flashed in his eyes. "I'm not ready to let this go yet."

Neither was she.

She could handle this. Manage a little more time with Nick. More sex. More walking on the wild side with a man who couldn't—wouldn't—hurt her on purpose. Right? "Pizza sound good?" She climbed into the driver's seat.

He got in the truck on his side. "As long as there's nothing green on it."

"Not a pepper guy?"

"Not a pepper guy."

And not a relationship guy, but she quickly extinguished the thought or she'd ruin the happy hum in her body. Her keeping him at arm's length had backfired. Her emotions *were* involved. But she'd mastered shutting them down after Michael and she could do it again. Only this time she'd get to keep happy memories.

A few minutes later, they got to the Stop 'n Go so Nick could pick up his car. He walked around the hood of the truck and leaned his arms over her open window. She took her hand off the steering wheel to play with his fingers. "I'll follow you to your house," he said.

"Okay."

"Nick?"

He turned his head. Cass looked over his shoulder. Paige stood behind him, a curious look on her face. "Hey, sorry to interrupt but I noticed you and wanted to be sure you were still heading to Rocco's tonight?" Paige's eyes slid to Cassidy. "Hi, Cass."

Cassidy smiled at…Nick's Thursday night date. She slipped her fingers from Nick's to get going, but he squeezed her wrist. *Stay*.

Nick straightened to give his full attention to Paige. "Sorry, no. I'm not going to make it."

"Oh?" Paige said with a definite question mark.

"I never actually said I'd be there. You threw out the invitation and assumed I'd be available, but I'm not. Have a good time, and congratulations again."

Paige stared in disbelief. Despite her self-centered personality, she didn't get rebuffed very often, if ever. "I guess I'll see you around then. And thanks." She cast a quick inquisitive glance at Cassidy before she turned on her high heels.

"It's okay if you want to—"

"Really?" Nick challenged, his eyebrows raised. "It's really okay with you if I go to some work thing with Paige instead of going home with you?"

Cassidy slowly shook her head. "No," she mumbled.

"Good. Because if you blew me off for someone else, I'd want to break the guy's face."

That was the nicest thing any man had ever said to her. A closed mouth, overjoyed smile took hold of her face.

Nick blessed her with the grin that made even the most standoffish women want to get friendly. "I'll be right behind you."

"Later, too?" she prompted before he'd stepped too far away.

"While you're on your hands and knees."

She sank into the car seat, squeezed her thighs together. A few suggestive words from him had her throbbing with excitement. Fired up.

Falling hard for him whether she liked it or not.

Chapter Ten

NICK SCANNED THE hotel ballroom full of photographers seated for dinner. More people filled the space than he'd anticipated and it bothered him once again that he'd had to meet Sid rather than arrive together. If the guy she'd wanted to avoid had tried anything...Nick shook off the unwelcome thought, continued his search. The lively conversation and laughter grated on his nerves for no other reason than he'd yet to locate his date.

Not a date, he reminded himself. This is a simple return of favor for saving his ass at the bachelor auction. After tonight they had no reason to keep in touch any more than they did normally. Sid was a complication he didn't need or want. Stick to simple, short-lived, he reminded himself for the hundredth time. He'd learned the hard way that anything more than that resulted in loss.

The numerous crystal chandeliers lighting up the room sparkled, but not half as brightly as the gorgeous face that smiled at him when his gaze landed on the right table. Nick hated clichés, but swear to God, time stood still as he soaked Sid in.

She wore an ice blue gown with small cap sleeves and a neckline that pushed her breasts up. She'd swept her long hair to the side in a loose knot under her right ear. Her lips shimmered with pink gloss.

"If you're looking for an empty seat, I'll make room for you next to me for the rest of the night." A woman to his side offered. And it was an offer, her voice carrying the unmistakable pitch of interest he'd heard numerous times over the years. There was a time he would have been flattered and flirted back, but the only voice he wanted in his ear tonight was Sid's.

He turned to the attractive woman. "Thanks, but I've got someone keeping a seat for me."

"Lucky girl."

"Luck's got nothing to do with it." He stood there because of a business transaction. Which, given his gruff response, bothered him even more than he'd cared to admit over the past three weeks. What a selfish idiot he'd been to put it put that way.

"Oh, well if you find yourself wanting a new seat mate then, come find me."

"I won't need any new company," he said, turning his head back in Sid's direction. "But thanks for the offer. Have a good night."

"You, too," the woman said before taking off across the room.

Nick took a step, but stopped when he noticed Sid no

longer sat at the table. He searched left to right and back again, but no luck. His heart rate sped up. Why was his pulse pounding? She had to be around somewhere.

"You're late." The soft whisper floated over his shoulder, raising the hairs on the back of his neck in awareness.

"You're stunning."

"Good answer."

"It's the truth." He did a one eighty. Seeing Sid up close, he almost high-fived the waiter who walked by. Cassidy took graceful beauty to a whole new level. But beyond her exterior, she had an inner glow about her that he wanted to bask in. She outdid the sun *and* the moon. What would happen if he stayed in her orbit?

He took her hand to lead her out of the ballroom.

"What are you doing?" she asked with reluctance.

Yeah, he shouldn't be dragging her away from her event, but he needed a minute alone with her. A minute to tell her this wasn't impersonal for him. That he wasn't here because he owed her one. He *wanted* to be the man by her side tonight.

"Having you to myself long enough to do this."

She stiffened and sucked in a surprised breath when he cupped the back of her head and kissed her, *hard*, but a second later she melted against him as he pushed his tongue inside her mouth. His free arm went around her waist. Her arms went around his neck. The hot, deep, compulsive kiss rooted him in a really fantastic moment. Something only her kisses did. The press of her hand to his tuxedoed chest made him reluctantly break contact.

With her high-heeled shoes, they stood nose to nose. Her well-kissed lips enticed him to lean in for another taste, but she leaned back to say, "That was unexpected."

"Because we're in public?"

"Yes."

"Hard to help myself when you look the way you do." He angled his head to brush his lips against her neck, inhale her scent. "And smell the way you smell."

"You look pretty handsome yourself."

"I'm glad you think so. Should I behave myself from now on?"

She searched his eyes. Looking for his true feelings? He didn't share those anymore, but he'd hauled her out here to concede something. "I will if you want me, too," he said. "But it's no hardship making this a real date, Sid."

"Nick…" Something caught her attention over his shoulder, but before anything else was said, she palmed his nape and smashed her mouth to his. No words were good. He could handle no words *all* the time. The kiss ended—far too quickly—when someone behind him cleared his throat.

"Jesse, hi," Sid said, acting surprised by his arrival, but Nick had a feeling the brief molestation of his lips had to do with her catching a glimpse of the guy she'd been worried about seeing. Nick had no problem with that. Sid could be as demonstrative as she liked.

"Hey, Cassidy. I was hoping I'd run into you tonight." Dude definitely looked at Sid with undisguised appreciation.

"I thought I'd see you here," she said amicably.

Jesse cut a quick glance his way so Nick extended his hand. "Nick—"

"Oh, sorry. Nick this is Jesse. Jesse, Nick."

"Sid's boyfriend," Nick added, complicating matters by making his and Sid's relationship more serious than it needed to be to keep Jesse at bay. But for some reason Nick felt staking his claim without any room for misinterpretation the best strategy here.

"Nice to meet you," Jesse said. Then to Sid, "I didn't know you were seeing someone."

"It's new," she mumbled.

"So there's a chance I can steal you away." Jesse's rude and inappropriate candor made Nick want to introduce his fist to the guy's face.

Instead, Nick put his arm around Sid to bring her flush against his side. It killed him to feel the tension in her body. Her anxiety had him reconsidering the fist thing. If this douche was so out of line with her *boyfriend* present, what kinds of things had he said to Sid in private?

"Not a chance in hell," Nick said.

"Hey, man, I was just joking. But can you blame me? Look at her."

Nick *was* looking at her. And by the way his stomach churned, he didn't want anyone else to.

Jesse seemed to realize his inappropriate compliment was an asshole thing to say. He opened his mouth to continue, but Sid spoke up first.

"Thanks, Jesse, but you know what? I'd really appreciate it if you kept your thoughts to yourself. I've tried to make it clear I'm not interested, and if you can't respect my wishes then you need to keep your distance."

"Cassidy, I didn't mean—"

"Maybe not. But what you think is charming can be really off-putting. I have no problem with remaining friends, but only if you accept nothing will happen between us whether I have a boyfriend or not."

"I apologize if I came off the wrong way."

"Thank you." She turned in Nick's arm. "You ready to go back inside?"

"In a minute," he said.

Jesse smartly took that as his cue to leave and with a "See you later," walked away.

Nick faced Sid. "Nice job. You didn't need me here at all."

She gave him a smug smile. "You're right. I didn't need my *boyfriend* to help me put Jesse in his place. What in the world possessed you to say that? I mean, I know I asked you to help me, but that wasn't what we agreed on and I didn't like being caught off guard. I'm already..." She trailed off.

"You're already what?" Feeling as unsure about things between them as he was? He wanted to protect Sid, but as she'd just proved, she could take care of herself. So what did he want from her? What did he want to be…to her?

More than nothing, but less than something popped into his head. Because bottom line, he couldn't commit, couldn't open up his heart again.

"Outside my comfort zone." At his frown she added, "I'm not really big on these black tie events and would have skipped it if not for the award."

"Back up. What award?"

"I'm being honored tonight for one of my photographs."

"Why didn't you tell me?"

Her shrug told him plenty. She didn't tell him because he didn't mean anything special to her. He'd agreed to come tonight to help keep her safe, not celebrate her achievements. The distinction stung.

He'd done this to himself. Gotten closer to a woman than he ever had before and pushed her away at the same time.

"Congratulations." He kissed her cheek.

"Thanks. So we should probably go sit down now." She laced her fingers with his to walk beside him back to her table. "I am really glad you're here with me tonight," she said quietly as they took their seats.

Throughout dinner Nick rarely stopped touching her. He couldn't help himself. This was their last night together. Her skin was soft and warm and every time his fingertips brushed the back of her neck, she shivered. No one asked the status of their relationship. No one questioned their familiarity with each other. Conversation flowed with ease. And hearing her receive accolades from her peers filled him with even more admiration for the woman he couldn't stop thinking about.

"Here I've been following some guy on Instagram who posts pictures of turtles when I should be following you," he whispered in her ear.

"Turtles?"

"They make me happy." *Not nearly as much you do, though.*

She sighed with delight, like a child might when given some top-secret information. "Sea or land?"

"I'm an equal opportunity turtle guy." He rubbed his nose along the slim column of her neck. "God, you smell good. Your pheromones are a definite mating call to mine." Had he really just said that? Christ. Something was wrong with him.

"So talk of turtles also turns you into some Animal Planet weirdo?" She teased.

"Thank you for that."

"You're welcome."

The rest of the evening carried on without any further awkward words on his part. Sid received her award and despite her nerves, looked beautifully poised as she gave her thanks. They hadn't discussed staying overnight at the hotel, but as they followed the crowd out of the ballroom, a two-hour drive at ten o'clock at night sounded terrible.

That and he didn't want to say goodbye.

Not yet.

With Sid's hand securely inside his, he walked them toward the registration desk. She didn't say anything, understanding what he meant to do. Recognizing this was the end to their arrangement, but not quite the end of them.

She let him go to make the reservation while she stood across the foyer. He kept one eye on her the whole time. Watched her undo her hair and shake her head to let the long waves fall down her back. Noticed her teeth sink into her bottom lip. Caught her green gaze and held it when she met his regard.

Room key in hand, he took her arm and they headed for the elevators. He wasn't sure if he could trust his voice so continued to stay quiet. She broke the silence with, "Thanks for reading my mind."

"Yeah?"

"As amazing as you look in that tux, I haven't been able to stop thinking about seeing you out of it."

"Did you picture me in my underwear when you were accepting your award?" He moved his arm to the small of her back as he leaned forward to press the button for the elevator.

"No! If I'd done that I would have screwed up my speech."

"You're a liar, you know."

"*What?*"

"You were a pro up there. And you had our entire table hanging on your every word. I think your comfort zone is whatever you make it."

She smiled at him. The unmistakable joy in her expression hit him in the chest and below his belt. Seeing her happy stirred more than one reaction inside him.

"I think I have you to thank for a lot of my new found confidences."

They stepped inside the empty elevator. Nick pressed the button for the twentieth floor. As the doors slid closed, he turned Sid so her back faced his front. Her quick, aroused intake of breath filled the small space.

He swept her long hair over her shoulder. Then he placed his hands on her waist and kissed the back of her neck. Softly. Gingerly. Like time didn't exist. Like he could spend hours right here, loving the smooth, delicate flesh of her throat He dropped delicate presses up to her earlobe, reversed direction, and slowly moved his lips down, inhaling her scent and getting harder with every swipe of his lips and tongue on her skin. Her head tipped to the side when he kissed the sexy curve where her neck met her shoulder. His hands slid to her stomach, traveled up to her breasts. He palmed them through the material of her dress while he continued to lavish her where her pulse started to pound. Heat beat a path down his spine when she quivered and moaned in pleasure.

"I want your mouth all over me," she murmured.

"Done."

"And I want you in my mouth."

"You're killing me, babe," he said, his open mouth brushing across her upper back, goose bumps rising in the wake of his kisses.

The elevator came to a stop. They both dragged in a breath.

Nick hustled them down the hallway, anxious to have one last night wrapped up in each other. They moved clumsily into the room, hands seeking, mouths colliding. And then because he couldn't tell her, he showed her how much he cared.

CASSIDY TIPTOED AROUND the dimly lit room trying to locate her panties. She could leave them, but the thought left a bitter taste in her mouth. It wasn't like Nick would see her to return them. Well, she supposed he could, but it was better to make a clean break without any reminders of their steamy night together. Their temporary involvement was over now and next week he'd leave for a new job in Idaho…or somewhere else. She had a new life waiting for her in Los Angeles once she and Rowan figured out all the particulars. Life had them going in different directions. Literally.

It was hard enough to say goodbye to her hometown, the house she'd grown up in, and the people she'd known her whole life. Saying goodbye to Nick, well…

She'd tried to stay ambivalent about her new ties to him, but she should have known sharing her body with him would make that impossible when she had a brand new crush on him.

Okay, way more than a crush. But she didn't want to love him.

God bless-ed. Where the heck had he flung her thong to after pulling it off with his teeth? She'd been too stuck on watching him work his way down her legs to notice, but the room wasn't that big.

And once again her eyes landed on Nick's sleeping form. He was flat on his back, the sheet at his waist, one arm above his head, the other across his rock hard abs, his hair a mess from her fingers. His chest rose and fell so peacefully, she envied him the sleep he'd found.

After two hours, she'd had enough staring at the ceiling and decided the best way to say good-bye was not to say it all. Which made her a coward. But that was better than having him notice she'd had the best time of her life with him this past month.

Or letting him see that she had fallen hopelessly in love with him.

The important thing was he'd helped get her over her self-imposed hump—or whatever it was that had kept her from fully letting go. She could be wild, have fun, and not get hurt in the process.

Mostly.

Nick was the exception.

Because she'd relinquished all of her inhibitions and let herself go too far.

She looked away from the sleeping, sexy man who cared for her, she knew, to find her damn underwear. *There they are.* Hooked over the corner of the chair. She lifted her dress and pulled them on. Picked up her strappy heels, small clutch, and her award, and with one more look at Nick over her shoulder, slipped out of the room.

The drive home in the middle of the night took no time and too much time. Alone with her thoughts on the dark, almost deserted highway she thought about her life, her choices. For the first time ever, she was the person she wanted to be. Not the overly cautious person her parents had tried to force on her. Not the cynical person her college boyfriend had turned her into. But someone secure in her own skin, a woman who wanted and was capable of love and adventure and deserved it.

So why tears were streaming down her face, she didn't know. She blinked a bunch of times to stop the waterworks, but it didn't do any good. She started to cry harder, the ugly, runny nose, can't-catch-your-breath kind of crying she hated. Her body shook with her sobs. A chill settled over her shoulders. Blurry spots marred her vision and she should probably pull off the road, but she pressed on the gas pedal instead. She wanted to be home in her bed with the covers pulled up to her chin.

She hadn't expected this to be so hard. Or hurt so much. There had always been an end date, but she'd foolishly put it out of her mind. If she didn't think about it, maybe it would cease to exist, right? Wrong. With every brush of his fingers, kiss on her lips, and stroke inside her body tonight, Nick was saying his good-bye.

Walking into her bedroom a short while later, her eyes were still miserably wet. She swiped the back of her hand under her nose and sniffled. The pressure in her forehead warranted pain relievers, but suddenly she was too tired to take even one more step. She got undressed, leaving her gown on the floor at her feet, and crawled into bed.

The sheets were cold, but then so was her skin, so it didn't feel quite so disagreeable getting comfortable. Less than a minute later, she'd warmed up. A minute after that, sleep thankfully took her.

"Oh, thank, God."

Cassidy stirred, vaguely aware of someone saying something. She sensed the brightness in the room so knew she'd slept and morning had arrived, but she was in that place between sleep and consciousness that felt so cozy, she didn't want it to end yet. Or ever.

It felt like floating on a bed of feathers. Her mind was blank and—

The bed dipped. "It's time to wake up, Cinderella." And bounced. Someone was dipping and bouncing on her bed.

Rowan.

"Okay, okay," Cass grumbled, her throat dry. She opened her eyes and squinted at her best friend. "I'm awake. Can you please stop that now?"

"Yes," Ro said, hopping off the bed. She walked around to Cass's side to sit on the edge of the mattress. "I'm happy to see you're alive."

It always took Cass a few minutes to come fully awake, but what in the world was Ro talking about? "Why wouldn't I be?"

"True. I wasn't really worried, but Nick was."

That got Cassidy's attention. She pushed up, sitting against the headboard and hugging an extra pillow to her chest to cover her bareness. "What are you talking about?"

"You've got some 'splaining to do, chica. Not that I hadn't already put the pieces together. But why didn't you just tell me when I asked you what was going on with my brother?"

"I didn't think…I wasn't sure…"

Rowan rolled her eyes. "Whatever. You'll tell me everything in a minute. Let me send a quick text to Nick to let him know you're okay." She thumbed several words into her cell, looking quite pleased with herself, then tossed the phone onto the middle of the bed. "He called me a half hour ago asking if I'd heard from you. When I said no, he cursed like a sailor"—she grinned—"and told me the very condensed version of what had happened and that he was worried you'd driven home in the middle of the night."

"I did."

"Obvs."

"What's the big deal?"

"The big deal is Nick kind of lost his mind thinking it was selfish of you to do that when it wasn't safe. What if you'd fallen asleep at the wheel? Driven off the road into a ditch? Gotten a flat tire and some weirdo stopped to help you."

"He called me selfish?" Anger and hurt coiled into a tight knot behind her ribs. She'd never been called that before. Hadn't once considered her actions last night selfish.

But now that she thought about it, they were. They so, so were. She'd convinced herself in those hours she'd laid awake that the best course of action was to sneak away. That way, she couldn't be disappointed by what Nick did or didn't say in the morning. She could save herself from her own misguided expectations.

Keep some small nugget of hope alive.

All this consideration, though, had been directed at herself.

"Hey," Rowan said, no doubt noticing her dour expression, "you're not selfish. I know this because I know you. And I know you did what you had to do to be okay. That's called self-preservation. Nick's still just sensitive from the sub fire. Especially with people who are important to him."

Cassidy lifted her eyes to meet Rowan's.

"Now tell me the whole story and then I promise you coffee."

"I always planned to tell you."

"I know."

Some things were harder to share than others for Cass, but luckily since this was Rowan and they were talking about her brother, Cass didn't have to go into any details about the sex. When finished, Cass was glad for the weight lifted off her shoulders. Speaking about Nick was sometimes painful, but it was therapeutic, too. And with Ro's warm blue eyes saying all the right things, Cass spilled every appropriate piece of information.

"You're in love with him," Rowan said supportively.

For a split second Cass thought about saying no, but Ro would see right through it. "Yes. But it doesn't matter."

"Because?"

"He doesn't love me. And before you get mad at your brother, it's okay. I knew what I was getting into. He made it clear from the beginning that emotions had no part in what we were doing. I'm not sorry any of it happened, and you have to promise me you're not going to say anything to him."

"But—"

"No buts. I mean it. The subject is closed." It had to be in order for Cassidy to keep moving forward.

"But the way he smiles at you. He does—"

"*Rowan.*" Cass was not above putting her fingers in her

ears and la-la-la-ing if Ro didn't get off the topic.

"Fine." She got to her feet. "I'll just grab us some caffeine and be right back. Wait until you hear what I did last night." With a mischievous slant to her smile and sparkle in her eyes she left the room.

"Hurry!" Cass called after her, always happy to hear about her best friend's exploits.

And selfishly, relieved to have the distraction.

Not five minutes after Rowan had left, though, the doorbell rang. Thinking Ro had come back, Cassidy opened the door without bothering to look through the peek hole. Something she never did anywhere but in Marietta.

"Hey, did you—"

"Hi, Sid."

Cass froze. She opened her mouth to speak, but nothing came out. Nick stood in front of her wearing his black tuxedo pants and wrinkled white button down, the collar open extra wide at the neck like he'd dressed quickly. His hair was a hot mess. Weariness creased the corners of his eyes. She swallowed the lump in her throat. He'd driven straight from the hotel to see her.

"Can I come in?"

No. Yes. This was one of those sweaty-palmed moments when she didn't know what the right answer was. She'd left him in the hotel room for a good reason—to protect herself. So having whatever conversation he wanted to have with her seemed less risky with him on the other side of the threshold.

Until his eyes took a slow tour down her body and back up. The quietness of his perusal, like he wanted to savor one last look, undid her. She resisted the urge to pull her oversized Old Navy T-shirt down to cover more leg as her body flooded with heat. Her mind went blank, save for the lethally handsome man in front of her. He had a way of looking at her that made her forget her own name.

"Okay," she said softly, stepping aside to offer him entrance.

The only rooms that still had furniture were the kitchen and her bedroom. She led him to the safer option and took a seat at the small, round pine table. He sat across from her, pushed up his shirtsleeves. She stared at his strong forearms before remembering her manners and glancing back up. "Can I get you something to drink?"

"No, thanks. I just came by to…"

Cassidy waited for him to fill the silence, her foolish thoughts racing to, *I just came by to tell you I love you.*

"To…?" She prompted.

He ran his hand over the sexy stubble on his jaw. "See for myself that you were okay."

Her ridiculous hope deflated faster than she could say, "I am." She wasn't. But she'd swallow her tongue before she admitted otherwise.

"I didn't like waking up and finding you gone."

"I couldn't sleep. Missed my own bed." And couldn't stand the thought of this conversation.

"If something had happened to you on your way home..."

"I'm not your responsibility, Nick." She fidgeted in her chair. God, being this close to him and hearing the concern in his voice was worse than fingernails on a chalkboard. Couldn't he see how much she just needed him gone?

"No, but you do owe me some common courtesy."

What? Anger rose up the back of her throat. "I wasn't trying to be disrespectful when I gave us a clean break."

He gave a slight shake of his head in disapproval. "That wasn't clean, Sid. It was sneaky and selfish. How would you have felt if the roles were reversed?"

She closed her eyes against the onslaught of regret—and his gorgeous blue gaze. He was right, but she wasn't the bad guy here, was she? She'd left to make things easier for both of them. Yet sitting across from the man she'd fallen for and not being able to touch him was incredibly hard.

"Exactly," he said. "You'd feel used."

Her eyes flew open. "That couldn't be further from the truth and you know it."

"So set me straight. Why'd you leave?"

"To avoid the uncomfortable morning after!" Of course he didn't get it. He didn't feel the same way about her that she felt about him. He never let his armor slip.

"Aren't we past that?"

Men are nincompoops, Rowan had said half an hour ago. Cassidy repeated the sentiment to herself as she smoothed her hands down her cotton shirt.

"Not this time." She countered, her focus falling to his hands atop the table. Hands that had been all over her body with skill and tenderness and devotion.

He reached for her. She scooted her chair back. If he touched her, she'd lose what tiny strides she'd made to move on.

"I'm a little lost here. Did I do something to upset you?" He dropped his arm to his side. "Because I enjoyed every second of last night and thought we'd wake up together and I'd buy you breakfast."

His mere presence upset her right now. "Then send me off."

"Send you off?" His voice held a bitter edge. Finally he was showing some emotion to match her own. "That's what you think of me?"

"I can't allow myself to think of you," she admitted, hating the way her voice cracked.

Their eyes met from across the table. She saw the ocean between them in his blue regard. "Sid, I was upfront with you from the start."

"I know, but it doesn't make this any easier. Not for me."

His gaze went somewhere over her shoulder like his mind had wandered off and he didn't know what to say. That right there told her everything. He couldn't give her want she wanted.

He slowly got to his feet. "I'm not sorry for the time we spent together."

Cassidy stood, too. She moved behind her chair, gripped the back. She needed the support to keep standing. "I'm not either. God, Nick. It was perfect. Every minute."

"So let's take whatever time we have left together and keep doing this." He stepped closer.

She held up her palm to keep him from taking a second step. "Now who's being selfish?"

"What does that mean?"

"*Really?*" Was her love for him not written all over her face? "You're not the least bit aware of my feelings for you? I left last night because I *had* to. I can't keep doing what we're doing knowing you're off to one place, I'm off to another, and you're fine with that."

"Sid—"

"Can you offer me more?" Her body shook with the words she'd been afraid to say. She knew the answer, but hearing it would cut the slivers of hope in the back of her mind. It was more than just the distance coming between them. His heart was closed off.

He threaded his fingers through his hair. "No."

"Then I'd like you to go now."

Despite his answer, he had the decency to look pained. "Goodbye, Sid."

She didn't reply. That one little word hurt too much to say back. She watched him walk away. When she heard the front door shut, she sank to the kitchen floor.

And cried the last tears she'd shed over Nick Palotay.

Chapter Eleven

SINCE WHEN DID his baby sister make him sweat like he'd run ten miles? "Jesus, Ro, cut right to the chase why don't you?" Nick said, two fingers at the collar of his T-shirt.

"That's what journalists do," she answered, her pen poised to write his response on her legal-sized letter pad. He'd told her he didn't want to be recorded, so she'd brought the large notebook instead. If her plan was to intimidate him, it was working.

Aside from that, he was damn proud of her.

They sat in the living room of their parents' house for this interrogation—interview—and only five minutes in, he wondered how much longer she wanted him for. He'd promised to treat her as a reporter, though, not his kid sister, and take the interview as serious as he would with a journalist from *Newsweek*, so that meant she had him for as long as she wanted.

"So?" She prompted.

Right. Answer the question. His sister had done her homework, which shouldn't be a surprise, considering she was hoping the article would get picked up by a newspaper in LA. Where she was moving. With Sid.

"Yes, two firefighters died when they fell through a hole left by removed deck plates during the fire."

"They were more than just first responders with you." Ro looked him right in the eyes when she spoke. "They were your best friends."

Fuck. "Yes."

Her gaze softened. "Losing one person on your team, let alone two, has got be incredibly difficult. How do you cope with that?"

Nick raked his hand through his hair. Since the accident, he'd thought a lot on that. Last week he'd sat down with Coach D for lunch to get some perspective, too. The man had lost his grandson, a tragedy no grandparent should face, and the older man had offered the final words Nick had needed to hear in order to close the two most painful chapters in his past.

"Suffering loss isn't easy and it's important to mourn. After that, acceptance makes you stronger but also kinder, especially with yourself, and that changes everything."

Ro lifted her head from her scribbles. "So, you're saying it's important to move on and not stay stuck on the pain?"

"That's part of it, yes." There was nothing he or any other firefighter could have done differently to save Jake and Alex. It was just their time. And for whatever the reason, it had been Sloan and their baby's time, too.

"The sub was undergoing an extensive overhaul at the

time of the accident. Was neglect on the part of the maintenance crew to blame for the explosion?"

"Absolutely not."

"But to keep costs down, spare parts from decommissioned subs are used in repairs. Should the navy continue to—"

"Ro."

"Yes?"

"I'm a firefighter. Not a commander or a politician. Can we keep to that?"

"Oh, sure. Sorry." She waved her pen in the air. "And, uh, I know you hate the personal questions, but it's part of my job to ask them."

"I know." He gave her a weak smile.

"Okay, so"—she straightened her back and glanced at her notepad—"is there a difference between firefighter Nick and off-duty Nick?"

The question threw him. He was always in protector mode, always aware of his surroundings, and ready to lend a hand without being asked. But since leaving the navy, he'd had a chance to stop feeling like he had to be on top of everything. He'd chilled out and taken himself less seriously. Remembered what it was like to be carefree.

The time off had been exactly what he'd needed before he ran himself into the ground. That, and a certain long-legged photographer who'd made him feel alive again.

"There is now."

"Can you explain?"

"Firefighting is in my blood, and that will never change, but I've learned to relax when I'm not working. Be spontaneous and drop my guard."

"And is there anyone special who has helped you reach this new state of being?"

Nick narrowed his eyes in warning. No way in hell was he talking about Sid during this interview. His sister knew it. He knew it. In fact, he'd told Rowan to drop the topic of Cassidy all together when she'd tried to bring up her best friend.

He'd walked away from Sid. It killed him to think he'd hurt her, but she'd asked for more than he could give. Time might erase the pain of loss, but he didn't want to risk feeling even one day of torment like that ever again. Three human beings—four counting the life growing inside Sloan—had been ripped from him. There was only so much a person could handle.

Shit. He'd been trying really hard not to think about Sid. But each day over the past week got harder than the last. He missed her. Ached for her. And now she sat front and center in his mind again.

"Next question."

"Come on, Nick. You're a gorgeous, unattached firefighter and single women are going to want to know about your love life."

He ground his teeth together. "My love life is private."

"So, you have one then?" She smiled at him like he'd walked right into that one.

Nick had known calling Rowan with his worry about Sid would come back to bite him in the ass, but he'd felt an actual pain in his chest when he'd woken at six AM in their hotel room and found her gone. Fear had slammed into him. He'd needed to do something and being a hundred miles away from home, he'd had to rely on his sister for help until he could see Sid for himself. He also knew Sid would tell Rowan everything the minute Ro had texted him Sid was alive and well.

Rowan put down her pad and pen and scooted to the edge of the couch, her back straight, her eyes determined. Great. She'd decided to go off the record. "Tell me how you really feel about love."

"I told you to drop it."

"Why?"

"Because there's nothing to tell."

She tilted her head to the side. "I think there is. And I think you should get it off your chest. It will make you feel better. I promise."

"I feel fine." At least he had up until two minutes ago when his tenacious, little sister turned their interview into a therapy session.

"Fine isn't good enough. I want you to feel over the moon happy."

"Get back to our agreed upon interview and I will be.

Otherwise, I'm walking."

"You promised," she said with a pout that, goddammit, worked every time.

He clenched his hands into fists. The high back chair that was usually his favorite place in the house to sit suddenly grew uncomfortable. "One question." He ground out.

"Could you love Cassidy?" Interesting how she'd said "could" instead of "do" because there was a distinction and she knew it.

"No." Hardest fucking word he'd ever said. Again.

"Because of your job?"

"That's two questions." But she'd pretty much nailed half of it on the head. He'd decided to take the job with the National Interagency Fire Center in Idaho and bottom line was his job came with danger he didn't want to subject anyone else to. If he could spare someone feeling the way he'd felt with loss, he would.

"Oh, my God!" Ro threw her arms up in the air. "You're such a cliché. Fireman loses his first love in a fire, loses two best friends, too, and thinks he can't love again because of some misplaced lone wolf thing to keep heartbreak to a minimum. Well, news flash, people lose their loved ones no matter what their occupation or how safe they play it. Shit happens. All. The. Time." She shook her head in irritation, her eyes blazed with anger. No. Disappointment. Which killed him. "Also? You're not sparing your parents or your sister or your friends their feelings, so why not close yourself off from them, too?"

"Rowan." He leaned forward to put a hand on her arm but she slid down the couch out of reach, picked up her pen and paper.

"She means something to you, Nick, and you're an idiot if you don't do something about it."

He'd done nothing *but* think about that something for the past five days. And without a doubt, he'd think about it for the next fifty years.

CASSIDY'S CRAVING FOR mac and cheese couldn't have come at a worse time. She tapped her foot on the tiled floor of Main Street Diner waiting for her take-out and willed herself not to look in Nick's direction for the tenth time in the last minute.

Oops. There her eyes fell again. She had zero willpower when it came to him. His black untidy hair, chiseled face and broad shoulders were to blame at the moment, so she cut herself some slack. She'd noticed her gaze wasn't the only one to land on him. Thankfully, he sat with a group of guys who kept him distracted from looking toward the diner's entrance. Not that he'd be aware of her if he were alone.

Guh. She turned her back to him and stared out the double glass front doors at the moonless night sky.

Rowan had told her he was leaving in three days. Seventy-two more hours and they wouldn't chance a meeting unless they both flew into Marietta for visits at the same time.

She closed her eyes for a moment and when she opened them, the diner had fallen into complete darkness. Cassidy heard Flo, the chef, curse from the direction of the kitchen. Paige, the owner of the diner grumbled from behind the register and said, "These darn power outages are really getting on my nerves. What good is the electrician if he doesn't fix the problem."

Then Cass heard something she'd managed to avoid for the past eight years, but which had been stamped into her memory whether she wanted it there or not.

The striking of a match. That distinct sound of the stick swiping across the box and catching fire.

Panic rose up the back of her throat, jagged and sharp, as the agony from Michael burning her flesh came roaring back. Rationally, she knew Paige was probably only lighting a candle, but that didn't stop the fear from engulfing her. Somehow she managed to swallow her scream as her fight or flight response kicked in and she rushed to escape, to get outside into the fresh air before anyone noticed she was having a panic attack.

Her skin too tight, her fear too overpowering, she slammed into the glass door of the diner when she pushed instead of pulled. Her forehead stung as she clawed at the door handle. Her heart hammered so hard in her chest she could barely breathe. She needed to get out of there.

"Cassidy?" Paige said. "You okay?"

She didn't answer. Couldn't. Not without giving herself away. She vaguely heard her name again—*Sid*—just as she got grasp of the door and tugged it open enough to scurry through.

The cool evening breeze slapped her in the face. A welcome strike that took the edge off her anxiety as she ran into the middle of the parking lot and opened her mouth to inhale large gulps of air back into her lungs.

"Sid." Only one person called her that. "Are you all right?" Only one person spoke to her with that tone of voice. The kind that tricked her into believing she was something more.

"Fine," she managed to say before she walked away on shaking legs.

Nick stopped her with a hand to her shoulder. His touch grounded her, took her lingering fear and shrank it. God, how she wanted to turn and bury her face in his neck, take comfort in his arms, and let him erase the rest of her misery.

But that wasn't how this worked. And she could take of herself.

"Talk to me," he said. "*Please?*"

She stayed still. Debating. He wasn't demanding she speak to him. He was asking her to keep him in the place where she let few in.

He dropped his arm. She silently counted to five and turned. She couldn't bring herself to look into his eyes so she focused a little right of his ear, catching the lights flickering back on inside the diner.

"Paige lit a match and the sound took me back. I haven't had a panic attack like that in a really long time."

When Nick didn't say anything, she continued.

"I used to get them a lot. Didn't even need an actual trigger because my mind would go there at the worst possible time. Right after the sound always comes the pain and the smell and then this feeling of being trapped and struggling and wanting to die to escape the unbearable—"

Nick pulled her against his chest, wrapping her inside his strong arms. She went willingly, grateful he'd initiated contact. The embrace didn't mean anything more than reassurance at a time when she desperately needed it.

After her heart rate slowed and all the sharp edges inside her softened, she pulled back and stared into his handsome face. "Thanks."

"Welcome." He turned his head to glance back at the diner.

"I'm really okay now. Please go back and finish your dinner. Oh, and uh, good luck with the new job."

His eyes settled back on hers, unreadable, and her heart stuttered, her stomach turned. He'd closed himself off from her, because of what had just happened or because they'd already said everything they needed to say to each other she didn't know, but she had to get away from him.

She'd laid herself bare to him, made herself vulnerable,

again, and it was obviously more than he wanted to deal with.

If she never saw him again that would be fine with her.

"Bye," she said, twisting around and practically jogging to her car.

"Sid, wait."

"Nick!" A guy shouted a short distance away. "You coming back in?"

Cassidy kept moving without a look back. She climbed into her car, fiddled with the key, and after a deep breath, started the car. Waited a beat.

No one stopped her.

God, she hated this. Hated feeling so messed up inside that just when she thought she'd found freedom from her past for good, she allowed it to be ripped away from her.

Worse, though, was the pain at seeing Nick. Having him hold her so lovingly. Then losing him again. She'd thought nothing could hurt her more than the burns on her back, but she was wrong.

The moment struck her as monumental. Something hurt more than her ordeal in college. And even though her heart was breaking, she had Nick to thank for making her feel again. She'd look back on this day and remember this moment as the one that prompted her to take action, to conquer her fear of matches. It was time to do this.

She drove straight to the liquor store. The older man behind the counter took care of her purchase, dropping it into a small brown paper bag so she didn't have to touch it.

Her palms were slick, the back of her neck hot when she walked into the kitchen of her house a few minutes later. She dropped the bag on the counter before she flipped on every light in the room, including the tiny one above the electric stove.

You're in control here, Cassidy. It can't hurt you. What happened to you was because of a person, not an object. An object that when used correctly can bring light into the world. Happy light. Hopeful light. Romantic light.

She stopped pacing to pull the lone candle from the cabinet above the microwave and placed it on the counter. The large square pillar was white gardenia. Cass loved the smell of gardenias at night.

With hands shaking, she opened the brown bag and lifted out the box of matches. She dropped them next to the candle like they'd burned her fingers.

Her heart thrashed around the inside of her chest. *This is so ridiculous.* They were stupid matches. But it wasn't stupid. She'd been told over and over again that she wasn't crazy to fear them after what she'd been through.

She reached around to her back to feel the scarred skin she lived with every day as a reminder that she'd survived. *What doesn't kill you makes you stronger, right?*

The matchbox glared at her. Mocked her. She scowled at it and then…then she laughed. She was bigger, stronger, smarter, than some wood sticks and she could do this. With a deep breath, she slid the box open and took out a match.

Dropped it. Picked it back up. Nerves rattled her, but she held on to her determination like it was a lifeline. She pressed the red tip to the side of the box and swiped. Nothing happened. *Open your eyes, Cass.* She tried a second time, focused on the task. This time a flame appeared. Her knees wobbled so she leaned against the counter for support as she stared, trance-like, at the tiny orange flame, colored blue at its base. She watched it burn down the stick, charring it black, until it almost reached her fingertips and she panicked and blew the flame out with a quick breath. A tiny thread of smoke billowed up, then disappeared.

With the match extinguished, so was the unease that had twisted her spine while she'd watched it burn. The awful smell that made her want to vomit also floated away. She'd done it. Sweat coated her back, but she'd done it.

She lit another match. And another. Each time got a little easier. She lit them all until she had one left to light the candle with. The flicker of light, calm and beautiful, and *innocent*, filled Cass with a sense of peace long missing from her life. She walked around the room to turn off all the lights so that only she and her white gardenia candle glowed.

Hours passed in the kitchen. She watched the candle burn, feeling the pain, heartache and fear latched inside her, finally unlock. Not all of her apprehension was gone. If she let them, her thoughts strayed to an unhappy place, but she was close. So very close to smothering her fear for good. She might never be one hundred percent over it, but knowing she could handle herself made all the difference. And when she couldn't keep her eyes open any longer and bent to blow out the flame, she smiled, thinking that on her next birthday she wanted to blow out cake candles for the first time in nine years.

Chapter Twelve

NICK THOUGHT HE could let go. Let Sid go without any further words between them, but he couldn't stop thinking about two nights ago outside the diner. The look on her face before she'd run away undid him. He had no idea what prompted her to take off like she did, especially after he'd held her in his arms. And it had felt *right*. So right that he'd planned to bail on his friends and take her somewhere to talk.

Her sudden dismissal under guarded eyes had stolen his voice. It wasn't just embarrassment over her panic attack that troubled her. She'd turned her back on him, and he'd gotten the message. They were through. He'd told her as much last weekend in her kitchen.

Only they weren't. Not when he couldn't sleep, plagued by dreams of her naked in tousled bed sheets with a shy smile on her face that took him to a better place. And not when she'd gotten past his defenses and done what he thought impossible. Taken his heart. He wasn't sure what to do about that, but he couldn't leave for Idaho tomorrow without telling her *maybe someday.*

Would that offer be enough for her? Because right now he still couldn't trust his feelings. But tomorrow...

His head fell back against the car seat. Hell, he'd already screwed with her emotions enough already, hadn't he? He'd deserved the brush off at the diner. But he couldn't stop remembering before that, when every time she looked at him he saw affection. Warmth. And he'd done nothing to discourage her feelings because they'd felt good.

She was right. He was the selfish one.

He braced his hands on the steering wheel. Leave or walk up to her front door? He'd come for a reason, to make sure she was okay after the candle incident, but he could do that with a phone call.

A tap on the passenger window startled him. He turned the key in the ignition and hit the power down button to lower the glass. An older man he didn't recognize put a hand on the open sill and smiled. "Nick Palotay, right?"

"Yeah."

"Read about you in the Courier. Nice article. Thanks for your service."

"No thanks necessary. It was an honor." Nick had gotten several pats on the back since Rowan's piece appeared in the newspaper. She had, too, which made the torture she'd put him through for two hours worth it.

"You've been sitting out here a while so I thought I'd check on you."

"I appreciate that." Nick's gaze jumped over the man's

head toward Sid's house. "I'm good."

"She's not home, you know."

"Sorry?"

"Cassidy," the man said, his eyes shrewd. "She left for Los Angeles early this morning."

Disappointment seeped through Nick's skin. She was gone? Already? Rowan didn't leave for LA for another few weeks.

"She'll be back in a couple of days. Still has some unfinished business to tend to before she's gone for good." The old guy paused, then glanced down at the passenger seat. "Those for her?"

"They were." Nick had never given a woman flowers before, but the multi-colored bouquet of roses had caught his eye at the stand on the side of the road so he'd stopped to buy them.

"Want me to leave them inside for you? You could write a note."

He could. Maybe list the things he lo-liked about her. He smiled inside. She'd call him on a note like that, wouldn't she? "You've got a key?"

"Live right next door. I promised her folks I'd look after her whenever she was here and after the house when she wasn't."

"That's nice of you"

"Everyone needs looking after. And Cassidy, well I'm guessing I don't have to tell you how special she is. I'm going to miss her when she's gone."

So am I. "Tell her I stopped by, would you?"

The man gave a barely-there shake of his head and stepped away from the window. Nick couldn't be sure, but the old guy looked let down, his lips pressing onto a tight line. "I'll do that."

What else was Nick supposed to say? If his sister couldn't drag it out of him, then Sid's neighbor had zero chance. Although for a split second there, Nick had thought about spilling his guts and asking for some advice. But with he and Sid heading to different states, and her needing more of a commitment from him, what was the point?

"Thanks," Nick said, glad to know Sid was okay and apparently moving forward. That was what he truly wanted for her—a happy future.

NICK HIT THE snooze button one last time before stretching his arms over his head and rolling out of bed. The hardwood floor cool under his feet, he took a few steps to stare out the window of his apartment in Boise. Like it had for the past two weeks, the blue sky and mountain range in the distance rivaled the beauty of Marietta, but every time he'd stepped into the fresh air, something felt wrong.

He shrugged off the thought like he always did, showered, dressed, and grabbed a cup of coffee.

An hour later, he stood in a classroom with twenty pairs

of second grade eyes looking up at him with curiosity and...hope. A recent tragedy in the community had landed him here. The new guy, whose special skills and training were welcome additions in the field, and whose personal experiences made him the perfect person to address accidents and loss.

Nick folded himself into a tiny plastic chair on the round colorful rug. Nerves didn't usually grip him, but this crowd, with their small, expectant faces, had him rubbing the back of his neck, hoping he didn't screw up.

He talked about his job. He talked about fire safety and prevention. He talked about himself, with far more ease than he'd anticipated. Kids apparently brought out the motor-mouthed boy of his youth. When finished, he asked if anyone had any questions. Every child's hand, but one little girl's, shot into the air.

Talk about an interrogation. They asked great questions. Smart ones. Funny ones that lessened some of the tension children should never be faced with. The morning had turned out to be his favorite one since arriving in Idaho.

The little girl with light brown hair and big green eyes, who coincidentally reminded him of Sid when she was young, hung back when the rest of the kids ran outside for recess. With a nod from the teacher, Nick knelt beside her at her desk.

"Hi, Becca."

She continued to work on her drawing without answer.

"That's a really nice picture. I bet the person with the big ears is your little brother."

That got her to peek at him for a second. The picture of a family—her family Nick guessed—tore a hole through his gut. She'd lost her dad in a fluke accident during a controlled wildland fire.

"My sister used to draw me with a mouth that was wider than my face."

"Did she call you big mouth?" Becca asked curiously.

"She did." Nick caught a tiny smile from the young girl. It put one on his face. "Know why?"

"You tattled?"

Nick shook his head. "No. I could eat a double cheeseburger and she couldn't. It made her really mad."

"I like grilled cheese."

"I like that, too."

Becca flipped to the previous page on her drawing pad and tore out the single piece of paper to give to him. He stared at the picture, touched by what he saw.

"This is me?" The blue eyes, dark hair, and fireman's hat gave him the hint.

She nodded without looking at him.

"Thank you."

"Becca," the teacher said, "I'd like for you to go play outside for a few minutes while I walk Mr. Palotay out."

Becca put her crayon down and stood. "I'm sorry," she whispered to him before turning and walking out the open classroom door.

He swallowed the giant knot in his throat and watched, as a little girl who had suffered far more than was fair, still have the grace to say those two little words to him. He should have said them to her.

In that moment, one person, *the* person, who meant everything to him flashed through his mind for the thousandth time. *This is all wrong.* Nick wasn't where he wanted to be. He was fucking miserable in Idaho because Sid wasn't with him.

Each night, he'd fallen into bed physically and mentally satisfied and made excuses for why satisfied was good enough. He'd skipped Friday night beers with a bunch of the guys twice, turned down a date with the nice barista who served him his weekend coffee, and when Rowan called to check in on him, lied and said he was great.

Lying pissed him off. Going through the motions from sun up to sun down was no way to live. Feeling more alone than he'd ever felt before sucked.

He was in love with Sid and had been too chicken shit to do something about it.

Well, someday was today, right now, and for the rest of his days if she'd let him. Like a fish over dry land, Nick needed Sid to breathe.

He folded his drawing, grateful to Becca for reminding him to treasure each day, waved good-bye to the kids on the playground, and took off to let his supervisor know he'd made a mistake.

CASSIDY TOOK ONE last walk along the river. Snow no longer topped the mountains of Paradise Valley and she idly wondered if she'd miss it before shaking her head. Of course she would. Marietta would always be home, always hold a special place in her heart.

Nowhere did Mother Nature better.

And nowhere held so many memories.

Spring's warm breeze rustled the leaves in the trees and rippled the steel blue water. A pair of paddle boarders floated toward her. On one of the boards, a black Lab sat up front, looking like the king of the world. Cass grinned and moved to the edge of the water to snap some pictures.

She planted her feet and lifted her camera from around her neck. *Do not fall on your butt. There won't be a handsome fireman to help you up.*

Cass zoomed in on the dog. She didn't normally take animal shots, but this was too good to pass up. Sensing her, she guessed, since she'd never had a dog, the Lab looked at her. A split second later, the canine dove into the water and started swimming toward her.

"Toby!" the teenager on the board shouted.

Toby didn't turn around. Cassidy liked dogs, so stood her ground in case help was needed to get the dog back on the board.

"Sorry, lady. I think your camera set him off," the young

guy called out.

"No worries," Cass yelled back.

Only as Toby reached the embankment, there was no easy ground for his paws to gain purchase with all the dense vegetation. Toby's owner paddled closer, kept calling the dog's name, but Toby seemed to want out of the water.

Cass knew if she tried to help Toby up, she'd probably end up in the river. If she didn't have her camera with her, she'd happily go for it, but the dog wasn't in danger, just excited to see her, and Toby's owner was almost within reach now.

"Need some help?"

Cassidy jumped. *That voice.* She'd heard it in her head every day for the past several weeks. Without waiting for an answer, Nick filled the space beside her. His arm brushed hers.

"Hey, boy," he said, easily bending down to spin Toby around so the dog swam away from the riverbank and back to his owner where he easily climbed back onto the board.

"Thanks, dude!"

"No problem," Nick said, wiping a few splashes of water off his face.

Cassidy took a big step back. She didn't know what to do with Nick's surprise appearance. Run? Stay and act like seeing him again didn't make her heart race? Crap.

He straightened. Turned a panty-melting smile on her. And then in some weird, slow-motion pantomime lost his footing and fell on his rear end, cursing all the way down.

She tried really hard not to laugh. "Are you okay?"

"I think I just bruised my tailbone."

"Ouch. Give me your hand. I'll help you up."

As usual, when his midnight blue eyes met hers everything around her faded away but the two of them. The air crackled when their hands met.

"Hi," he said, once back on two feet.

"Hi."

"Follow me to safer ground?"

Cass didn't think anywhere safe with Nick, but she nodded because, with her curiosity piqued, she'd follow him to wherever he wanted to go.

Back on the trail, she was surprised to see a tandem bike left unattended. Even more shocked when Nick said, "Take a ride with me?"

"Nick, what's going on? Why aren't you in Idaho?" *If I get on that bike what does it mean?*

He cupped her cheek. "I promise I'll explain. Come on." He straddled the front seat, looked over his shoulder and waited.

For weeks she'd tried to get over him and failed.

She climbed onto the back seat. They rode in silence under the powder blue sky until they reached a small picnic area with two tables. A red-checkered tablecloth, wicker food basket, and bouquet of red roses sat atop one of the tables. Nick parked the bike and hopped off. Standing beside her, he held out his hand. She took it as she dismounted, then keeping their fingers intertwined, he led her to the decorated table.

"You planned a picnic for us?" Her voice cracked, giving away her nervousness. She ran her free hand down the side of her pants to dry the perspiration on her palm.

"I did."

She sat first. He took the spot beside her, straddling the bench so he faced her. What she dared to read in his expression turned her inside out. *Yep, that's my heart wanting to claw its way into your chest so it can hump yours.*

Rather than touch her again, he gripped the edges of the wood seat.

"It's lovely." Stop thinking about heart humping and focus on food.

"Sid."

"Yes?" She forced herself to keep her eyes locked on his.

"I'm sorry," he said with so much sincerity she could feel it on her skin. "I'm sorry for walking away, and I never should have let you go that night at the diner. I want to be the guy who's there for you. I want to help you get over your fear of matches and flames. I'm the perfect guy for it actually."

She wanted to focus on the perfect guy part, but instead she said, "It's okay."

"It's not. I—"

Cass pressed two fingers to his mouth. "I'm glad you

didn't come after me." She'd needed to help herself that night. "Because," she continued when lines creased his forehead, "it gave me the opportunity to work through it on my own." She told him everything, a sense of accomplishment and pride stealing over her again.

"You're amazing."

"Thanks."

He brushed a wisp of hair away from her temple. "I'm about to do something I've never done before so bear with me?"

She'd bear anything for him. Everything. She regretted having him and losing him because she'd needed all or nothing. If he sat here to ask for any part of her, she'd be his again. They'd figure out a way to make this work. "Is there fried chicken in that basket?"

"There is," he said around a smile.

"Okay, then. Go ahead."

"I hated Idaho. It was a nice place and the job was good, but I was missing the one thing I realized I can't live without."

"The ocean?" He'd been a navy guy for the past twelve years. It made sense.

"I do miss that. Not sure what I was thinking with the landlocked work, but, no, that's not it." His gaze moved around her face before settling on her mouth. He leaned forward, brushed his lips against hers. "I missed you. You matter most to me, and I don't care where I am as long as

I'm with you. Life isn't always fair. But I don't have a life if you're not in it."

Heart jackhammering in her chest, she managed to whisper, "Meaning?" She needed him to spell it out; afraid to trust the path her thoughts had taken.

"I quit the job in Idaho. I don't have to figure out my next career step yet. And when I do, I want it to be something we decide on together. We've never really talked about my job and it comes with risks."

Her body shook with gratitude and love. So much love it overwhelmed her. She'd never ask him to give up something he was passionate about, but his asking her to help with his decision calmed any fears that might come up. She'd read Rowan's article and knew how devastating losing his friends on the sub fire had been. Add in Sloane, and he'd never wish that feeling on someone else. She knew down to her bones he'd take extra care of himself if he had someone waiting for him.

"I love you, Sid. You're my home. The person I want to share every day with starting right now. Please tell me I'm not too late. It wrecked me to think I'd never kiss you again or hold you in my arms and whisper how beautiful you are."

Cassidy flung her arms around his neck and kissed him. A messy and wild kiss she poured all the admiration and affection she had for him into. When she came up for air she took his face in her hands and said, "You're not too late. I love you, too."

He crashed his mouth against hers. It was his turn to show her how much he cared and he succeeded spectacularly. Her lips were sore, her head woozy, her heart full when he pulled away several minutes later.

"I will never get enough of that," he said.

She turned to straddle the seat and put her hands on his thighs, canted her head to nip at his earlobe. "Me either."

"I also want to strip you naked and come inside you against this table."

A rush of warm wet heat settled between her legs. "What are you waiting for?"

He did some curse-groan-mumble thing under his breath. "I didn't surprise you out here to do that." Taking both her hands in his he brought them to his mouth, kissed her knuckles. "This was supposed to be romantic and a chance for me to fully apologize."

"Apology accepted. And I'm sorry, too."

"When do you fly to LA?"

"Tomorrow."

"I'll catch a flight, too. I meant what I said. I want to be where you are. I'll find a place to rent and—"

"Don't."

"Shit. I'm moving too fast. Making assumptions I shouldn't."

"No. It's not that." She squeezed his hands, kept them firmly in hers. "If you're okay with it, you could move in with me."

His eyes twinkled. “Thanks, but I don’t think that would go over very well with Rowan.”

“She’s not going to be there.” At his frown she added, “She’s staying in Marietta. You haven’t talked to her?”

“Not in a week. Is everything okay?”

“Yes, and I’ll let her fill you in on her good news. So…it happens that I have this really great condo all to myself.”

“Done.”

Bursting with happiness only touched the surface of the emotions swirling inside Cass. “Yeah? You know I travel a lot, right?”

“I could come with if you want. Other times, I’ll keep the bed warm.”

“I love both those ideas.”

“I love you. And plan to show you how much every single day.” He wrapped his arms around her waist and lifted her closer so she straddled his lap. “How about I feed you the fried chicken and we get out of here?”

“Or…”

“Or?”

“We could take it with us and eat it in bed.”

Nick jumped to his feet with her in his arms. “That’s a much better plan, but fair warning. I may forget about the chicken.”

Cassidy giggled. “Me, too.”

The End

The Bachelor Auction Returns

Bachelor for Hire by Charlene Sands

Falling for Her Bachelor by Robin Bielman

Seducing the Bachelor by Sinclair Jayne

Weekend with Her Bachelor by Jeannie Moon

For more stories from The Bachelor Auction, check out...

The Bachelor Auction Series

Bound to the Bachelor by Sarah Mayberry

Bachelor at Her Bidding by Kate Hardy

The Bachelor's Baby by Dani Collins

What a Bachelor Needs by Kelly Hunter

In Bed with the Bachelor by Megan Crane

One Night with Her Bachelor by Kat Latham

Available at your favorite online retailer!

About the Author

When not attached to her laptop, USA Today Bestselling Author and RITA Finalist, Robin Bielman loves to read, take hikes with her hubby, and frequent coffee shops. A California girl, the beach is her favorite place for fun, relaxation, and inspiration.

She loves to go on adventures, and has skydived, scuba dived, parasailed, gotten lost in the wilderness (and only suffered a gazillion bug bites for it) hiked to waterfalls, and swam with dolphins. In her spare time she also tries to put her treadmill to good use while watching her favorite TV shows, indulges her sweet tooth, and plays a mean game of sock tug of war with her cute, but sometimes naughty dog, Harry.

Writing is a dream come true, and she still pinches herself to be sure it's real. She lives in Southern California with her high school sweetheart husband and loves to connect with readers.

Get the scoop on Robin, her books, and sign up for her newsletter on her website at robinbielman.com.

Thank you for reading

Falling for Her Bachelor

If you enjoyed this book, you can find more from all our great authors at TulePublishing.com, or from your favorite online retailer.

Made in the USA
Middletown, DE
01 March 2022

62007056R00123